Chestnut Hill
Helping Hands

Lauren Brooke

■SCHOLASTIC

With special thanks to
Catherine Hapka

Scholastic Children's Books
An imprint of Scholastic Ltd
Euston House, 24 Eversholt Street
London, NW1 1DB, UK
Registered office: Westfield Road, Southam, Warwickshire, CV47 0RA
SCHOLASTIC and associated logos are trademarks
and or registered trademarks of Scholastic Inc.
Series created by Working Partners

First published in the UK by Scholastic Ltd, 2008

Copyright © Working Partners, 2008

ISBN 978 1407 10845 2

British Library Cataloguing-in-Publication Data
A CIP catalogue record for this book is available
from the British Library

The right of Lauren Brooke to be identified as the
author of this work has been asserted by her.

Printed and bound in Great Britain by CPI Bookmarque, Croydon
Papers used by Scholastic Children's Books are made from
wood grown in sustainable forests.

1 3 5 7 9 10 8 6 4 2

This is a work of fiction. Names, characters, places, incidents
and dialogues are products of the author's imagination or are used
fictitiously. Any resemblance to actual people, living or dead,
events or locales is entirely coincidental.

www.scholastic.co.uk/zone

Chapter One

"What *is* your problem?"

Dylan Walsh froze in the act of pulling on her left paddock boot. The muffled but distinctly cranky voice had come from the direction of the human-sized lump huddled beneath the set of Italian linen sheets on the twin bed on the other side of her dorm room. A second later the lump sat up and pushed back the sheets, revealing itself to be Dylan's roommate, Lynsey Harrison.

"Sorry," Dylan said, yanking her boot on. "I was trying to be quiet."

That was true, though if pressed Dylan would have admitted it had nothing to do with consideration for Lynsey. On paper the two girls seemed to have a lot in common – they were both eighth-graders at Chestnut Hill Academy, came from well-off families, and shared an interest in horses and fashion. Despite all that, they got along about as well as oil and water. Dylan considered Lynsey a prissy, spoiled snob, while Lynsey never hesitated to make it clear that she found Dylan brash, reckless, loud, obnoxious, vulgar and not nearly as funny as Dylan thought she was. Given a choice, neither would have chosen the other as a roommate – if anything, they would have lived in different dorms, or better yet different countries! Unfortunately, the school's room assignments had left them no choice in the matter and so they were stuck with each other for three long semesters.

Still, on this particular morning Dylan had tried to be quiet; she really had. It was a gorgeous late-October Saturday, bright and crisp with the leaves showing a riot of autumn colours and a pleasant hint of frost in the air. In other words, the perfect day for a trail ride in the wooded Virginia hills that surrounded the boarding school. The last thing she wanted was to be forced to deal with Lynsey on her way out of the room and risk spoiling her fantastic mood.

Lynsey pulled off her lavender-scented silk eye mask and tossed it on her nightstand. "It's bad enough I have to wear this thing because your stupid night light is brighter than the Cape Hatteras lighthouse," she complained, brushing her long blonde hair back over one slim shoulder. "Am I going to have to start wearing ear plugs too, if I want to get my beauty sleep?"

"I don't know," Dylan said, quickly gathering her own springy red hair into a rather untidy ponytail and winding a band around it with a snap. "But I totally understand your concern, Lynsey. You definitely can't risk losing *any* beauty sleep."

With that, she grabbed her second paddock boot and

scooted out of the room. Just as the door closed behind her, she heard Lynsey snort and say, "Very mature, Dylan."

Dylan grinned and paused just long enough to pull on her boot, then continued down the hall with her laces untied. No, even Lynsey couldn't spoil her mood today!

She whistled as she headed for the room shared by two of her best friends, Lani Hernandez and Honey Harper. "Rise and shine!" she called out, letting herself in without bothering to knock. The room was dark, so she flipped the switch by the door. "We're wasting daylight!"

A groan came from the direction of Lani's bed. "Am I having a nightmare, or is Dylan standing there yelling at us at the crack of dawn on a Saturday morning?"

Honey opened her eyes and sat up, her face flushed with sleep and her shoulder-length blonde hair tangled. "Good morning, Dylan," she said, stifling a yawn. "Playing alarm clock today, are we?"

Dylan plopped herself down on the edge of Honey's bed. Then she bent over to tie her boots. "You got it. Plus I got to annoy Lynsey on my way out, so that was a bonus."

That made Lani sit up and grin. "Really? What did you do – tuck a little fresh horse manure under her pillow?"

"No! But that's a great idea for tomorrow morning." Dylan leaned forward and lifted one hand for a high five. "Did I ever tell you I like how you think, Hernandez?"

"Ditto, Walsh." After trading high fives, Lani jumped out of bed and padded over towards her dresser, barefoot and wearing her usual nightclothes – a pair of cut-off sweatpants and her favourite Denver Broncos T-shirt.

Honey looked concerned. "You two are joking about the horse manure, right? You'd have to be barmy to mess about with Lynsey so soon after all that stuff with the All-Schools show."

Dylan knew exactly what stuff she meant. Recently Lynsey and her best friend, Patience Duvall, had spread rumours about one of the Chestnut Hill ponies being fed something suspicious at a horse show. It was nonsense, of course, but it had caused a lot bad feeling at the time. Dylan didn't want to think about that right now when she was in such a good mood.

"Barmy?" she echoed playfully instead, mimicking Honey's British accent. "Could I get a translation, please?"

"I know that one," Lani put in, glancing up from rummaging around in her sock drawer. "She's saying you're nuts, Walsh. Bonkers. Stark raving loony."

"Oh, that." Dylan shrugged. "So what else is new?"

Honey giggled. "All right, then what *did* you do to Lynsey this morning, Dylan?"

"I didn't do anything to her. As usual, it was all in Lynsey's tiny mind. I just couldn't quite manage to get dressed without waking her up, even though I was trying to be quiet."

"Really?" Lani looked dubious. "Last time I checked, 'quiet' wasn't exactly your middle name, Dyl."

"I swear! I was tiptoeing around like a mouse." Dylan

shrugged again. "Trouble was, I was still making too much noise for Princess Lynsey. You know – pushing back the covers, standing up, putting on my socks, breathing… So she wakes up and starts ranting away about my night light, blah blah blah."

"She should know better than to encourage you to get rid of that night light." Honey pulled her legs out from under the covers and hugged them to her chest, resting her chin on the knees of her floral-print cotton pyjama bottoms. "After all, it was *her* fancy designer sunglasses you squashed that time last year when you forgot to turn on the night light before bed."

"Really?" Lani said. "What happened?"

Honey giggled. "Dylan ended up tripping over her own slippers when she got up for a midnight trip to the bathroom."

Dylan smiled sheepishly. She, Lynsey, and Honey had all shared a room the previous year, and she remembered the incident well. She'd come away with a bruise on her knee, and Lynsey had come away with a pair of flattened Dolce & Gabbanas and an even lower opinion of Dylan than before.

"Yeah, the night light never seemed to bother her last year," she said. "It's only this year that she started being such a drama queen with the special herbal-scented imported eye mask and everything, acting like she can't sleep." She shrugged. "But she's got no room to talk. I mean, the smell of her face cream keeps me awake, and you don't see me going to sleep with a clothespin on my nose, right?"

"Maybe you should," Lani suggested as she pulled on her jeans.

"Maybe I will." Dylan stood up. "Anyway, now that you two are awake, I'd better go get Mal up."

"Doubt you'll have to," Honey said, climbing out of bed and stepping into her slippers. "She and Alexandra are both early risers."

Sure enough, when Dylan reached the room their friend Malory O'Neil shared with another eighth-grader named Alexandra Cooper, she found the door ajar, Alexandra nowhere in sight, and Malory bent over her school books at her desk.

"Knock knock," Dylan sang out, hurrying in. "Feel like a quick trip to the barn this morning?"

Malory looked up and blinked at her. "Oh. You're awake," she said, glancing at her watch. "Is it noon already?"

"Ha ha, very funny." Dylan rolled her eyes. The girls' usual Saturday routine was to get up early enough to visit the horses and help with the morning chores down at the stable yard before heading to the dining hall for brunch. However, even Dylan had to admit that she wasn't always as enthusiastic as she could be about mucking out stalls first thing in the morning. "No time to sleep in today," she added. "Not when there are ponies to ride and fall colours to enjoy! What do you say?"

Malory pushed back from the desk, stood up and stretched. "I say a visit to the barn sounds perfect," she said. "I've been staring at these stupid equations for so long that my brain is totally fried."

Soon all four friends were at the barn greeting its residents, who were spending nights in their stalls now that it was getting cooler. "Happy Saturday, Morello," Dylan chirped as she let herself into her favourite pony's stall.

The part-Welsh skewbald nudged at her, looking for treats. Dylan fished around in the pocket of her jeans, finally coming up with a peppermint she'd swiped from the dining hall. As soon as Morello heard the crinkle of the wrapper, his ears pricked forward so alertly that their tips almost touched.

Dylan laughed. "You sure recognize *that* sound, don't you, boy?" She unwrapped the sweet and fed it to him.

As the pony crunched down on the treat, Dylan glanced around at her friends. Across the aisle, Lani was patting Colorado, the spunky buckskin gelding she normally rode. Lani had ridden Western a lot back home in Colorado Springs, and the buckskin pony could go either English or Western style as easily as she could. Next to Colorado's stall was Tybalt's. The slender thoroughbred cross had come to Chestnut Hill the previous year as a nervous, overly reactive wreck and had almost been sent back. But Malory had made him her special project, and now the two were a great team. They'd had a setback recently when the gelding had been diagnosed with Lyme disease, but he had recovered well and was just about back to normal. At the moment Malory was performing some T-Touch style moves on him, moving her fingers in small circles on his glossy bay coat to soothe him.

Dylan couldn't see Honey, but she knew exactly where she was – a little farther down the aisle with Moonlight Minuet, better known as Minnie. She leaned out over the stall guard to catch a glimpse of the pair, smiling when she spotted them just in time to watch Honey wrap her arm around the pretty grey mare's neck, and see Minnie nuzzle Honey's shoulder gently in return. Minnie technically belonged to Dylan – or rather, her parents. A few months earlier they had offered to buy Dylan a new show pony, since she'd outgrown her old one, Tiptoe, who was now a school pony at Chestnut Hill. However, Dylan had decided she had little interest in working with any pony but Morello, and she knew that Honey adored Minnie, who was about to be sold and taken away from Chestnut Hill for ever. So she'd talked her parents into buying Minnie from her old owner, Patience Duvall, keeping the pony at Chestnut Hill and leasing her to Honey.

If I do say so myself, that had to be my best scheme ever, Dylan thought proudly. She was famous – some would say *in*famous – for concocting schemes and pulling pranks. *Nobody deserves the perfect pony more than Honey, especially after everything she's been through in the past year or two*.

Dylan grimaced. Not only had Honey moved from England to the United States, leaving her pony Rocky behind, but her twin brother Sam had been diagnosed with leukaemia at almost the same time. Fortunately, Sam had fought the disease and won; he was currently in remission and preparing to start at a nearby boys' boarding school, Saint Kit's, next semester.

Just then Dylan felt a sharp nudge in her back. "Hey!" she said with a laugh, turning to find Morello staring at her. "OK, OK, you're right – I'm supposed to be paying attention to you." She reached up and scratched under the pony's thick forelock. "Feel like a trail ride this afternoon, boy? Maybe a nice, long canter through some fallen leaves?"

The pony blinked at her, which she decided to take as a yes. Realizing she hadn't yet shared her trail-riding plans with her friends, she ducked under the stall guard and stepped into the aisle.

Before she could go any farther, there was a commotion at the far end of the barn. Glancing curiously in that direction, Dylan saw Joanna Boardman and Lucy Price emerging from the tack room with their arms full of saddles and pads, a couple of bridles hanging off each of their shoulders. Both girls were seventh-graders and members of the school's Junior Jumping team, along with Dylan, Lynsey and team captain Malory.

"What are you guys doing?" Dylan called to them. "Planning to ride four or five ponies at once?"

Joanna responded with a rather distracted laugh. "Nothing like that," she said breathlessly. "Ms Carmichael asked us to help groom and tack up eight of the quietest ponies." Ali Carmichael was Chestnut Hill's young, energetic, talented Director of Riding. She was also Dylan's aunt and Morello's owner. She'd taken the job at the school a little over a year earlier after the previous Director, Elizabeth Mitchell, had left to take over the riding programme at the Alice Allbright Girls' School, one of Chestnut Hill's nearby rivals.

"Yeah," Lucy put in. "There's a group from some kind of kids' home coming later for a riding lesson."

"Really?" Honey leaned out of Minnie's stall, looking interested. "What sort of home do you mean? Like a care home?"

Malory had come out into the aisle by now as well. "Probably Cheney Manor, right?" At Joanna's nod, she continued, "It's a live-in facility in Cheney Falls for troubled and orphaned kids." Cheney Falls was the nearest town to Chestnut Hill, and Malory lived just the other side of it. "My dad's store donates shoes every year. It's a really great place. Kids without families stay there while they're waiting for adoptive homes, and there is also a bunch of kids who still have families but can't live with them for whatever reason – illness, parents in jail or on drugs, stuff like that."

"Oh, wow." Dylan tried to imagine what it would be like to be in that kind of situation. In a way, it sounded a little like boarding school, and she loved boarding school. But she couldn't imagine not being able to return home to Connecticut to see her parents during summers and holidays, or knowing that her family was just a phone call or email away the rest of the time.

"Right," Lucy said. "And a bunch of those kids are going to be here in less than two hours to ride, so we'd better get started checking this tack and then grooming ponies."

"Need some help?" Lani offered.

"I think we're all right, thanks," Joanna said. "Alice and Jennifer are on their way to help out. Anyway, Ms Carmichael asked us to take care of it, so we'd probably better handle it ourselves."

Dylan held back a smile, remembering how important she and her friends had felt the first few times Ms Carmichael had asked them to help out around the barn. Sometimes seventh grade seemed a long time ago!

"OK, sounds like everything's taken care of around here," Lani said, patting her stomach. "We might as well head to brunch before all the French toast is gone. Ready?"

"In a minute," Dylan said distractedly.

Hearing about the visit from the Cheney Manor kids had made her realize she'd better reserve their ponies for that trail ride now, before they were otherwise spoken for. Being privately owned, Minnie wouldn't be a problem, and of course Tybalt was still far too skittish to be used by anyone but a very skilled, sensitive and confident rider – in fact, he was rarely ridden by anyone but Malory. Morello and Colorado were among the more forward and athletic equines in the string and thus unlikely to be called upon for the Cheney Manor job when there were more sedate ponies around, but if any of the regular Chestnut Hill riders decided to sign up for a nice afternoon hack or a little extra jump schooling or something…

"Be right back!" Dylan called to her friends, hurrying towards the exit.

Soon she was knocking on the door of her aunt's office, a converted stall in the European-style stable block across the yard from the main barn. Ali Carmichael was sitting at her desk making notes on her calendar, but she glanced up at her niece's entrance.

"Morning, Dylan," she said. "Everything OK over at the barn? I asked the seventh-graders to start getting some ponies ready."

"They're on it," Dylan reported. Then she explained why she was there.

Ali nodded. "It's a great day for a trail ride," she agreed. "And the ponies have been working hard lately – they could use the chance to get out in the open and stretch their legs." She stood up and jotted a note on the chalkboard near the door. "Consider your usual ponies reserved."

It wasn't until they had sat down with their brunch trays in the dining hall that Dylan finally got a chance to tell the others about the trail ride plans. "Not only is it absolutely perfect riding weather, but we haven't really had a chance to blow off steam and just have fun since the last show," she explained, digging into her scrambled eggs.

The other three girls exchanged a look. "That sounds awesome, Dylan," Lani said. "But we talked about going into town today to shop for Halloween costumes, remember?"

"Oh." Dylan blinked, a vague memory of some such plans floating through her mind. "Um, was that a definite thing? I guess I sort of forgot."

"We already arranged to meet the boys at noon," Malory said.

Dylan knew that "the boys" were Malory's boyfriend Caleb, Honey's crush Josh, and Honey's brother Sam, who liked Lani. The first two were students at Saint Kit's, and of course Sam would be joining them there in just a couple of months – in the meantime, his family lived close enough to allow him to visit easily.

"It'll be fun," Honey assured Dylan. "Maybe we can go for that ride tomorrow instead."

Dylan forced a smile. Most of the time it didn't bother her one iota that her friends all had boyfriends while she didn't. In fact, she found the matchmaking and the gossip involved in her friends' love lives endlessly entertaining. But now, for once, she found herself feeling a bit left out – not to mention disappointed as her visions of the perfect Saturday afternoon trail ride faded away.

"Actually, maybe you guys should go on to town without me today," she said. "I don't want to be a fifth wheel. Or wait…" She paused just long enough to do a quick mental count. "Technically I guess it would be a seventh wheel."

"Oh, but you have to come!" Honey cried, looking genuinely disappointed.

"Yeah," Lani put in, reaching for the syrup. "We need your creative mind to help us come up with cheap but totally spooky costumes for the Adams dorm Halloween party next week."

Dylan laughed. "I have faith in you, Hernandez,"

she said. "You can come up with something awesome without me. Maybe."

"Are you sure you don't want to come, Dylan?" Malory asked, still looking concerned. "Like Honey said, we could do this today and then ride tomorrow."

"I'm sure," Dylan assured her. "You guys have fun. And be sure to keep track of all the smooching you do with the boys today – I'll be waiting to hear all about it when you get back, and you know I like lots of details."

"Oh, please," Malory muttered, while Lani rolled her eyes and Honey turned red.

Dylan grinned. "Details, girls. Details," she reminded them.

Chapter Two

An hour later Dylan was back at the stable. Her friends were in their rooms changing for their day in town; they would be leaving shortly to catch the bus to Cheney Falls.

That left Dylan with a free afternoon and no trail ride – there was a strict rule at Chestnut Hill that trail riders had to go out in groups of at least three. For a moment Dylan had thought about either trying to convince her aunt to make an exception to that particular rule, or possibly trying to find another group to ride with. But she'd soon given up on both ideas. Ali Carmichael was a stickler for rules, especially those that involved safety. And a ride with someone else just wouldn't be the same.

She soon forgot about all that as she found the main barn in an uproar. Blaze, Tiptoe and Bella were in the cross-ties, and brushes and bits of tack were lying around everywhere. Most of the barn's usual residents had been turned out, including Morello, but tacked-up ponies were looking out from five of the stalls. The four seventh-grade volunteers were running around getting the ponies ready with help from Ms Carmichael and the two full-time stablehands, Kelly and Sarah.

"Need some help?" Dylan called to Kelly as she rushed past carrying a set of bell boots.

Kelly skidded to a stop. "Love some!" she replied breathlessly. "The van from Cheney Manor is due any minute now. Most of the ponies are ready, but we still need to do these three."

"Got it. I'll do Tiptoe." Dylan ducked under Bella's ties and walked up to her old pony. Tiptoe had been a talented competition pony in her day, but even then she'd always been quiet minded and kind, taking care of Dylan while teaching her as much or more than her trainers ever had. Now aged sixteen, the patient little chestnut mare was teaching Chestnut Hill's beginners just as much.

Dylan gave Tiptoe a hug and scratched all her favourite spots. Then she set about getting the pony ready, grooming her to a shine before tacking her up in her custom-fitted saddle and a clean pink square pad.

"Should we bridle them yet?" she called to Ms Carmichael when the pony was otherwise ready.

Ms Carmichael checked her watch, then glanced towards the doors at the end of the aisle. "Go ahead," she said. "I think I hear the van now. Dylan, can you stick around to help lead one of the ponies? Alyssa was supposed to help out but she's not feeling well."

"Sure, no prob." Dylan turned and gave Tiptoe a pat.

16

"Ready to go, girlie?" she murmured as she unhooked the ties and slipped on the bridle.

Moments later she and Tiptoe joined the parade of ponies and handlers walking out to the yard. When they emerged, she saw a somewhat shabby-looking minibus parked at the edge of the stable yard. The name Cheney Manor was painted on the side, and kids were already pouring out of it. One of the first out was a boy who looked about eight, with jet-black hair and lively dark eyes.

"Giddy-up, cowboy!" he shouted, racing towards Bella, who was at the head of the line of ponies.

"Howard, stop!" A woman jumped out of the van and chased him down, grabbing him by the arm before he could reach the ponies. "What did we tell you about running and yelling?"

"You're not supposed to say 'stop,' pardner," Howard informed the woman. "You're supposed to say 'whoa'."

Another Cheney Manor kid, a short African-American girl with thick glasses and pigtails, giggled. "You're crazy, Howard!" she cried. Then she glanced nervously at placid 13.2 hand Bella. "Wow, these horses are big! Are they Clydesdales? I saw some Clydesdales once at the fair."

Dylan grinned. She could tell these kids didn't know much about horses, but she had to admire their enthusiasm!

A tall, stick-thin girl with bright-pink hair had just climbed down from the van and was standing there with her arms crossed. "Don't be stupid, Charisse," she said.

17

"Even I know these horses ain't no Clydesdales, and I don't even want to be here."

"That's enough, Brittany," one of the other adults who had come with the kids said kindly but firmly. "If you really didn't want to be here, there are plenty of others who would gladly have taken your place. So let's work on the attitude, all right?"

Brittany rolled her eyes and shrugged, but didn't say anything else. She just wandered over to a patch of grass and started picking some small wildflowers that were blooming there.

OK, *so maybe they're not* all *enthusiastic about being here*, Dylan thought, her gaze wandering from Brittany to another girl, small and skinny with a pointy chin, big hazel eyes, and straight shoulder-length brown hair falling over her face. She looked about ten years old and was clutching a small pink backpack. One of the adults had just helped her down from the van, but she seemed unwilling to step very far away from it.

The rest of the kids were drifting towards the ponies by now. Even pink-haired Brittany followed the others despite her earlier comment. Only the brown-haired girl hung back by the van, fishing for something in her backpack.

Dylan wondered if she'd even noticed that the others had moved on without her. "Hey," she called in a friendly voice. "Come on over and see the ponies – they're looking forward to meeting you."

The girl kept digging into her pack without so much as acknowledging Dylan's words. Wondering if she was purposely ignoring her or maybe just shy, Dylan cleared her throat.

"Hey, I'm talking to you!" she tried again. "You with the pink backpack!"

When the girl still didn't respond or even turn around, Dylan frowned, feeling a bit impatient. She could sympathize with a hyper kid like Howard, or even outspoken Brittany. After all, she'd been accused of being hyper and/or outspoken often enough herself! But if there was one thing she found frustrating, it was being ignored.

"Listen," she said, marching towards the girl with Tiptoe trailing along at the end of the reins. She reached out to tap the girl on the shoulder. "Nobody says you have to love riding. But now that you're here, you should at least give it a—"

"Oh!" the girl shrieked, whirling around at Dylan's touch. She dropped her backpack and jumped away, clearly startled.

One of the adults heard the shriek and came hurrying over. "It's OK, Casey," she said, at the same time making some fluid, elaborate motions with her hands.

Dylan blinked, belatedly realizing the truth. "Um, is she – is she deaf?" she asked the woman. "I'm sorry, I didn't know, I…"

"It's all right, sweetheart," the woman replied with a smile. "You had no way of knowing."

"Sorry," Dylan said to the girl, feeling terrible. Realizing that Casey couldn't hear that, either, she gave a big shrug and raised her eyebrows, trying to express herself non-verbally. The girl didn't respond, and Dylan glanced at the woman. "So if she's deaf, that means she can't speak either, right?"

"No, Casey can speak just fine – she uses American Sign Language. Watch this." The woman turned towards Casey and made more of the hand motions, speaking out loud as well for Dylan's benefit. "Come along, Casey," she said. "Time to go ride these ponies!"

Casey looked anxious, but nodded and made a quick sign.

"What did she say?" Dylan asked.

"She just said 'OK'," the woman replied. "Now, can you tell me which of these ponies is named Tiptoe? That's the one Casey is supposed to ride today."

"Oh!" Dylan glanced over her shoulder at her old pony, who was standing patiently behind her. "Um, you're in luck. This is Tiptoe right here."

She smiled at the girl, feeling clumsy and kind of stupid, as the woman translated what she'd just said. She hoped Casey wouldn't hold Dylan's behaviour against Tiptoe!

Soon the entire group was in Chestnut Hill's largest outdoor arena. All the jumps had been removed and the footing raked smooth. The only thing in the ring was a sturdy wooden mounting block. Each of the Cheney Manor riders had been fitted with one of Chestnut Hill's plastic schooling helmets.

After a quick explanation of what they would be doing, Ms Carmichael asked the pony leaders to help the students mount. One of the Cheney Manor adults was a rider herself, so she took over the pony Ms Carmichael had been leading while the Director of Riding stepped to the centre of the ring to keep an eye on everyone. Dylan shot Casey a friendly smile as the girl approached.

"Come on over," she said, waving her free hand to indicate for Casey to come closer.

As the girl eased towards her one step at a time, Dylan glanced around, wishing the woman who had translated for them earlier was still with them. But she was halfway across the ring helping Sarah hoist the wriggling Howard into Tudor's saddle. Dylan bit her lip. It looked like she was on her own.

"OK," she said. "Um, time to mount." She gestured upward towards Tiptoe's saddle, then pantomimed lifting her foot towards the stirrup. "Come on, looks like the mounting block is free." She waved for Casey to follow her.

Casey seemed to understand, walking with her and Tiptoe towards the block. When Dylan pointed at it, she stepped up and stood there.

"Great," Dylan said. She shot the girl a thumbs-up. If that wasn't a part of American Sign Language, she figured it should be! "Now lift up your left foot toward the stirrup and swing your right leg over Tiptoe's back. Er…" She trailed off as the girl just stared at her.

Dylan bit her lip. How was she supposed to teach her how to mount without explaining things verbally? She could demonstrate by mounting Tiptoe herself, but then she'd probably get in trouble for not having someone holding the pony…

Before she could figure it out, the woman who had helped them earlier came over. "Everything all right over here?" she asked cheerfully, signing at the same time to include Casey in the conversation.

After that, things went much better. Casey was soon in the saddle. The woman, who introduced herself as Jill, stayed close by as Dylan started walking Tiptoe in a big circle around Ms Carmichael, along with the rest of the ponies.

"All right, everyone," Ms Carmichael called out after giving the kids a few initial tips. "Now just take a few minutes to get used to the feeling of the ponies walking. If you have any questions, just ask me or your leaders, all right?"

Dylan glanced back in time to see Jill signing what Ms Carmichael had said for Casey. "Tell her if she has any questions, just speak up and ask me," Dylan offered. Then, realizing what she'd said, she blushed. "Er, I mean, not *speak* up, you know, but, um…"

Jill chuckled. "It's OK, Dylan. I'll tell her."

"Thanks." Dylan waited until Jill had finished signing. Then she clucked to Tiptoe. "Tiptoe used to be a show pony, so she's super well trained," she said, glancing over at Jill. "She's really sweet and calm, too, so she's great with beginners."

Jill nodded, then started signing to Casey again. Dylan couldn't help being curious about American Sign Language – ASL, as she knew it was often abbreviated. She'd learned a few basic signs years ago from episodes of *Sesame Street*, but didn't know much else about it.

22

She wished she could watch more of Jill's signing, but she had to focus on leading the pony.

"Anyway," she told Jill once she'd finished the latest set of signs, "Tiptoe has really smooth gaits. The basic gaits would be walk – that's what we're doing now, obviously – trot, and canter."

"All right, everyone," Ms Carmichael called out a moment later. "Let's halt, then all reverse at the walk, please."

"Ho, Tiptoe," Dylan murmured, and the pony immediately came to a square halt. "See that?" Dylan told Jill. "She's pretty good with verbal commands." She grinned. "Ms Carmichael says it's probably from listening to the announcer during all those classes back when we were showing together, since Tiptoe knew *I* probably wasn't paying attention."

Jill chuckled, then started signing to Casey as Dylan clucked to the pony and turned her in a smooth circle. Soon the whole group was walking in the opposite direction.

Dylan glanced back to see how Casey was doing. She was sitting up straight and looking pretty good, though her heels had crept up.

"She's doing great," Dylan said to Jill. "She just needs to remember to keep her heels down. That helps anchor her whole leg and will also make it easier to signal to the pony when she gets to that point."

Jill nodded and turned towards Casey. Before she could start signing, Casey suddenly burst out with some muffled words. They were too garbled and quick for Dylan to understand, and she looked to Jill for help.

"I'm sorry, I didn't catch that," she said, surprised that Casey could speak verbally as well as through sign language. "What did she say?"

Jill smiled. "She said she's deaf, not invisible," she replied.

Dylan felt her face go bright red. She'd been directing all her comments to Jill, barely even looking at Casey except to check now and then that she was still in the saddle. It figured that Casey would feel as if she was being ignored, even though Dylan was actually addressing her.

"Sorry," she said, walking backward for a few steps so she could speak directly to Casey this time. "I'll try to do better from now on." She was aware of Jill signing beside the pony, but kept her gaze trained on Casey until the girl nodded and shot her a quick smile that was gone almost before it had appeared.

From then on things went much better. Dylan directed her tips and commentary to Casey, and Jill translated her comments as well as those Ms Carmichael made from the centre. By the end of the lesson, all the kids had walked, done a few balance exercises, practised steering a little bit on their own, and even tried a brief trot.

As she brought Tiptoe to a halt, Dylan looked back at Casey. "OK, time to dismount," she said. After a pause to allow Jill to translate, she went on. "Take both feet out of the stirrups, then swing your right leg back over the pony's hindquarters and slide down."

Soon Casey was on the ground. She stepped

forward and gave Tiptoe a pat on the neck, murmuring something to her that Dylan couldn't make out. Then she looked at Dylan and shot her a shy smile. She made a quick sign and mumbled something,

"Casey says 'thank you'," Jill said.

Dylan smiled at the younger girl. "You're welcome," she said. Then she glanced at Jill. "How do I say 'good job'?"

"Like this."

Jill showed her a pair of signs. Dylan watched carefully, then turned towards Casey and imitated the signs as best she could. Casey ducked her head and grinned bashfully. Dylan smiled back, feeling great. Maybe she and Casey hadn't started off on the right foot, but she was pretty sure they'd ended on it.

"…and then I learned how to say 'good job' in sign language. Like this, see?" Dylan demonstrated the signs Jill had taught her.

"That's brilliant, Dylan," Honey said. The four girls were having dinner together. "Sounds as though you had a nice time with those kids."

"I did," Dylan agreed. After the Cheney Manor kids had piled back into their minibus and left, Dylan had helped Ms Carmichael and the others untack the ponies and turn them out. Other stable chores and a visit to Morello in his pasture had kept her busy until it was time for the others to return.

"Well, I'm glad you had fun." Lani reached for the salt. "But I wish you'd been with us. We could have used your expert fashion advice on our costumes."

"Really?" Malory looked up from her dinner with a smirk. "Because the way you and Sam kept whispering and looking for any excuse to wander off together, it seemed like you didn't even remember the rest of us were there half the time!"

"Ooh, tell me more," Dylan prompted. "I want to hear all the gossip!"

Lani shrugged. "You won't get much here," she said. "The only reason Sam and I kept whispering and sneaking off was because we were plotting out dastardly Halloween pranks to play on the rest of you!"

Honey groaned. "Oh, dear. That much I can believe," she said. "I'm afraid my brother loves any excuse to make mischief!"

"Just like Lani," Malory put in. "That's why they're the perfect couple."

Dylan laughed as her friends continued to tease one another. For a second she wished she'd gone along on their trip to town – it sounded as if they'd had a lot of fun, as usual.

But she shook off the feeling almost immediately. No matter how much fun she'd missed in Cheney Falls, she wouldn't have missed meeting Casey, Jill and the other kids from Cheney Manor for the world.

Chapter Three

"All right, everyone, pipe down." Rosie Williams, the senior prefect for Adams dorm, raised one hand above her head. "Time to start the meeting."

Dylan looked up from her spot on the floor in front of one of the couches in the Senior Common Room. Rosie had called the entire dorm together for that evening's meeting, and the place was packed. The upperclassmen had snagged all the best seats for themselves, leaving the seventh- and eighth-graders to find spots wherever they could. Dylan had chosen a spot on the rug where she could lean back comfortably against the legs of Ansty van Sweetering, a sophomore member of the Intermediate Jumping Team, who was sitting on the couch with some friends.

"Hush up, people!" Lani called out when the hubbub continued despite Rosie's call for quiet.

Lynsey, who was perched on the arm of a chair nearby with Patience hovering beside her, rolled her eyes. "Bossy much, Lani?" she said haughtily. "I think you ought to let Rosie run the meeting, hmm?"

Normally Dylan might have made some sort of retort – she hated to let Lynsey's digs go unanswered. But tonight it didn't bother her. She was eager for the meeting to start. Every semester, each of the six dorms at Chestnut Hill held a fundraising event to benefit a charity of their choice. It was time for Adams House to decide what to do this semester.

"All right," Rosie said when everyone had finally settled down and turned to pay attention. "We all know why we're here, right?" She glanced at the dorm's seventh-graders, who nodded, having been filled in by friends from the other classes. "Good. Then I was thinking we'd start by deciding what charity we want to support this time. After that, we can come up with ideas for our event. So – any suggestions?"

Lynsey's hand flew up. "I have the ideal charity," she said confidently. "It's called Ballet in the Boroughs, and it benefits a ballet company in New York City."

"Ballet dancers?" Natasha Kapinsky, a junior, said dubiously. "Do they even need charity?"

There were a few giggles. Lynsey glared at Natasha. "Of course they do," she said icily. "My mother believes in supporting all the arts."

"Yeah," Patience spoke up. "Lynsey's mom hosted this really amazing banquet up in New York over the summer and raised tons of money."

"OK, we'll put the ballet group on the list," Rosie said diplomatically. "Who else has ideas?"

Faith Holby-Travis, a freshman and a talented cellist, raised her hand. "I think it's a good idea to raise money for the arts," she said. "But what about a music programme for disadvantaged students? I heard about one in Baltimore – I could find out more about it if you want."

"Or how about a therapeutic riding centre or something like that?" a junior named Polly Cooke called out.

"Don't you horse people ever think about anything else?" eighth-grader Razina Campbell teased good-naturedly. "I say we stick with people for once. Maybe a local homeless shelter or something?"

Suddenly Dylan had a great idea. "I know!" she cried, waving her hand in the air. "I've got the perfect charity for us to support!"

"Let me guess," Lynsey said to Patience in a stage whisper. "Fashion victims of America?"

A few people laughed, but Dylan ignored them. "It's Cheney Manor – they were just here earlier today so the kids who live there could have a riding lesson."

Razina groaned, shaking her head so vigorously that her beaded braids bounced. "There you go again with the horses!" she cried in mock dismay.

"No, listen," Dylan persisted, certain that she was on the right track. "It's this place where kids go when they have nowhere else to live – sort of like an orphanage, but they're not all orphans. Or maybe like a retirement home, but for kids, you know?"

"In England we called them care homes," Honey spoke up.

"That sounds interesting, Dylan," sophomore Hayley

Cousins said. "But a place like that probably has plenty of funding already through the state or something, right?"

"I'm not so sure." Dylan shook her head. "The van they came in was pretty beat-up looking. And I heard one of the staff say something about how more kids would have liked to come, so I'm guessing they're working with limited funds."

"I think this Cheney Manor place sounds awesome," Lani said. "Dyl was telling us about it earlier, and she said those kids were really grateful to come here and ride. It would be amazing to raise money to let them do more normal, fun stuff on the weekends." She shot a glance in Razina's direction. "Not *all* of it would have to do with riding," she added playfully.

Razina grinned. "OK, then I'm convinced. It sounds like a great idea."

Dylan glanced around the room. Other heads were nodding along with Razina's comment.

"Yeah, I've been to that place, and it does really good work," freshman Christy Snowdon spoke up. Her father was a US Congressman, and her parents kept a house in the Cheney Falls area as well as one in Washington. "My dad makes a donation to them every year, but he says they never have enough to fully support the programme or take in as many kids as need help."

"My dad supports them, too, through his store," Malory said. "I think it's the best possible idea for our charity."

Dylan shot her friend a proud glance. When Malory

had first come to Chestnut Hill, she'd been pretty sensitive about the fact that she was there on a riding scholarship and didn't talk much about her family or her life outside of school. Her single father, who owned a shoe store in Cheney Falls, could never have sent her to such an expensive school on his own. It didn't help that a handful of the other students, including Lynsey and Patience, insisted on making snide comments about Malory's modest family finances whenever they could. But Malory had become more and more open about her situation as time went on, and Dylan was glad she'd found her own voice to stand up for herself.

"OK, sounds like we have a few options." Rosie jotted a note on her pad. "So let's take a vote…"

When the votes were in, Cheney Manor won by a landslide. Almost everyone voted for it except Lynsey and Patience, who still seemed annoyed that their ballet group was being overlooked.

"Cheney Manor it is, then," Rosie said. "Maybe we can aim our event at raising enough money to buy them a second minibus so they can take more students on weekend outings. What do you think?"

"That would be awesome!" Dylan exclaimed. "Oh, and I almost forgot – Ms Carmichael said she could use more volunteers to help with the ponies when the kids come back for their next lesson. So anyone who's interested should let her know."

The discussion turned to what their fundraising event should be. Once again, ideas flew from every corner of the room. Aggninder Dillon thought they should do a 5K run. Faith suggested a classical music concert. Lani elicited snorts and laughter when she blurted out the idea to hold a Halloween parade and costume contest.

"Right," freshman Sydney Hunt said sarcastically. "I suppose you think we should plan and execute this fundraiser in less than a week. That might work – but only if new minibuses cost less than fifty cents."

"Hang on," Rosie spoke up as Lani stuck out her tongue at Sydney. "Maybe Halloween is out, but I'm liking the holiday idea. What about something for Thanksgiving or Christmas?"

"You mean like a Christmas Ball?" Lynsey said.

Patience's eyes lit up. "Ooh, what an amazing idea! We could hire out the town hall, and give a prize for the nicest gown…"

"If we send complimentary tickets to some of the best society people, I'm sure tons of other people would want to come," Lynsey said.

"Um, I don't know, you guys. If we need to hire some fancy hall and give away tickets and prizes, I'm not sure how much money we could actually raise for the charity," Helen Savage pointed out. "Maybe we should be a bit less…"

"Crazy?" Dylan finished helpfully.

Helen hid a smile as Lynsey and Patience scowled at Dylan. "Well, I was going to say ambitious," she said.

"Right," Rosie agreed. "Remember, this has to be something we can plan and pull off on our own, in between classes and activities and everything else we have going on."

"I know – we could chop down some of the evergreens in the woods behind the stable and sell them as Christmas trees," Lani joked.

Rosie rolled her eyes. "Or maybe not," she said. "But what about Christmas decorations? Maybe we could make ornaments and wreaths and stuff and sell them."

"I love it!" Razina looked excited. "My mom could probably get us some really cute African beads. Then we could market stuff for Kwanzaa as well as Christmas."

Dylan nodded eagerly. Razina's mother owned an art gallery in New York City and frequently travelled the world looking for unique pieces. Most of the beads in Razina's hair had come from Africa or other far-flung places.

"Perfect!" Dylan said. "If we come up with a few more really interesting ideas like that, people will be knocking down our doors to buy our stuff. We could raise a ton of cash for that minibus in no time!"

"Hmm." Lynsey didn't look entirely convinced. But she shrugged. "All right, I suppose that could work, as long as we make sure all the things we make are really classy and stylish. Maybe I can ask my mother if she has any contacts that might be interested in selling them for us – she knows the owners of all the most exclusive boutiques in New York and LA."

"That's very generous, Lynsey," Rosie said tactfully. "But we might be better off keeping this more local. You know – selling to other dorms right here at Chestnut

Hill, maybe calling on friends at other schools in the area..."

"We could set up a table at the weekly Holiday Fair at the mall," Alexandra Cooper suggested. "Lots of locals go to that, and I think it starts pretty soon."

"Great idea," Rosie agreed, jotting a note. "OK, does everyone agree on this general plan?" She glanced around and seemed satisfied with the number of nods and raised hands she saw. "Cool. Then I suppose our next step should be to decide what kinds of decorations we're going to make. Ideas?"

And again, suggestions came flying from all over the room. Susanna Janes wanted to make fresh pine garlands. Rachel Goodhart mentioned some wire stars she'd seen in a catalogue. Honey spoke up and suggested Christmas crackers.

"Christmas crackers?" Patience echoed, looking confused. "Wait, are we doing food, too?"

"No, not the type of crackers you eat," Honey explained with a smile. "The type of crackers I'm talking about are a sort of party favour – it looks a bit like a little package with bows on both ends. You pull the ends, it makes a noise, and there's a prize inside."

"Oh, I've seen those!" Lucy Weisbin called out. "My mom bought some through a British catalogue. It was fun! My little sisters really loved them."

A few other people nodded, though most still looked confused. Honey glanced around the room.

"They're not very well known in America, I guess," she said. "But they're very popular in England. We always, always have them on the Christmas table back home."

"Sounds like fun," Dylan said. "Do you think we could make them?"

"Absolutely," Honey said. "I've made them heaps of times."

"I've got another idea," one of the seventh-graders called out. "We could make ribbon wreaths. My aunt has one she puts on her door every year, and it's really cool." She paused. "Um, I'm not sure how to make them, though. I guess I could research it on the net."

Malory raised her hand. "My dad's store is right across the street from a really cute craft shop," she said. "Maybe we could get the owner of the shop to come in and talk to us. She probably knows how to make all this stuff, and might have ideas on marketing it, too."

"Perfect!" Dylan declared.

Lynsey looked less impressed. "A craft shop?" She wrinkled her nose. "Um, if we want to make any real money, we'll have to do better than, like, corn husk dolls or whatever."

"Yeah, really!" Patience rolled her eyes. "Talk about embarrassing!"

"My mother's decorator is doing our brownstone in a black, white and pink holiday theme this year," Lynsey went on. "He calls it turn-of-the-century Parisian chic. We should do that for our decorations, too. We could make some really nice-looking glass and crystal ornaments and matching wreaths with pink and black ribbons. Much classier than a mixed-up bunch of homemade-looking junk."

"Black, white and pink – for Christmas?" Polly Cooke said dubiously.

"Turn-of-the-century Parisian chic, huh? Hey, Dyl, where's your BlackBerry?" Lani said. When Dylan pulled it out of her pocket, Lani grabbed it and made a show of peering down at it. "Well, look at this! We're not in turn-of-the-century Paris – we're in twenty-first century Virginia! So I guess the pink Christmas thing is out."

Dylan grinned and caught the BlackBerry as Lani tossed it back. "Too bad," she joked. "I was looking forward to spray-painting the dorm's Christmas tree pink."

"OK, enough." Rosie tried not to smile too broadly as some of the others laughed and Lynsey fumed. "How about this – we can break ourselves into groups and each group can come up with one or two ideas they think will work. Meanwhile Mal and I will get in touch with the owner of the craft store and see if she's willing to advise us. Once we get her input, we'll vote on all the ideas and choose about half a dozen of them to produce."

"Sounds like a plan," Helen agreed, as just about everyone else in the room nodded.

"Great." Rosie stood up and tucked her notepad under her arm. "Let's tentatively plan to get together again next weekend. For now, meeting adjourned!"

"Ah, finally!" Dylan tipped her chin up to catch the afternoon sunshine, letting out a sigh of bliss and closing her eyes. She opened them a second later when Morello spooked at a bird flying out of a pile of dried leaves along the trail.

Honey watched Dylan lurch in the saddle, and grinned. As usual, sensible Minnie hadn't reacted to the bird at all. "You were right, Dylan. It's perfect weather for a ride like this."

"Definitely." Dylan gathered up her reins and looked back over her shoulder at Lani and Malory, who were riding side by side behind them. "Feel like a canter?"

"Ready when you are!" Lani declared as Malory nodded.

Dylan looked forward again and gave Morello a cluck and a nudge with her calves. The spirited pony didn't have to be asked twice. He leaped forward from a walk directly into a canter.

"Whoo hoo!" Dylan cried as they dove into the woods.

The trail was one they'd taken many times before. Broad and flat, with gentle curves and no large tree roots or boggy spots, it was the perfect spot for a canter. They went single file, with Morello in the lead, Colorado right behind him, and Minnie bringing up the rear. Tybalt could be excitable so Malory kept him in the middle as usual, staying a horse length or two behind Colorado and speaking softly to him the whole time.

Finally they reached the spot where the trail started to narrow and slope down, getting rockier as it neared the river. Reluctantly, Dylan brought her pony back to a brisk trot and then a walk. Morello let out a snort and tossed his head, seeming as disinclined as his rider to slow down.

Dylan gave him a pat, smiling as always at the thought of how perfect they were together. Then she glanced back at the others. "How was that?" she called.

"Wonderful!" Honey called back, sounding a bit breathless.

"Tybalt did really well." Malory leaned forward to pat the slender bay on the neck. "He's getting so much better at listening and not getting too wound up."

"That's because he trusts you, Mal," Lani said. "I bet nobody else at Chestnut Hill short of Ms Carmichael could canter him through the woods without risking life and limb."

Dylan turned around again, keeping an eye on the trail. She loved this area. They were now in the deepest part of the woods surrounding Chestnut Hill. The trees were so thick that the sun came through only in dappled spots here and there, and a riotous collection of birdsongs competed with the sounds of the river just ahead.

Soon they were splashing through the shallowest section of the river. Just beyond was the clearing known as Folly Glade. As she rode into the glade, Dylan glanced up at the tumbledown ivy-clad stone tower in the centre. It had been built in the nineteenth century in a deliberately ruined state, purely for decorative purposes, when the oldest part of the school, known as Old House, was a private home.

"Ah, here we are!" Honey announced as she brought

Minnie to a halt at the edge of the clearing. "Beware, girls, for there might be dragons about. Still, we must risk death by flames if we wish to rescue the handsome prince being held captive in yonder ancient tower!"

Lani laughed, letting her reins drop and swinging down from the saddle. "OK, Honey," she said. "You can invent all the romantic stories you want for this place. But you know as well as we do it was built by the original owners of Chestnut Hill just to give them something to look at."

"Oh, come on, Hernandez," Dylan said as she dismounted. "Even a science geek like you should at least try to have some imagination. It's way more fun to make up stories like Honey's than stick with the boring old real-life history."

Lani grinned. "True enough. Come on, let's go explore and check for that dragon."

Soon the ponies' bridles had been swapped for the halters the girls had brought along and they were tied to trees happily grazing on the last of the autumn grass in the clearing. The girls wandered towards the Folly.

It was a cool day, and it felt even cooler inside the damp stone circle of the tower's lower floor. Dylan tilted her head back and peered upwards. A crumbling stone staircase led to a partial floor halfway up the tower, though a sign on a chain across the lower steps warned that it wasn't safe to climb.

"Too bad we can't get up there," Dylan mused. "Bet it has a great view of the river."

"Don't even think about it, Dylan," Malory warned.

"You know your aunt will ban us from trail riding ever again if she finds out we ignored that sign."

Honey nodded. "Not to mention what Dr Starling would say if she heard about it."

Dylan knew they were right. She wasn't afraid of risking punishment under the right circumstances, but she supposed climbing the Folly probably wasn't worth it.

"Oh well," she said. "Even if we can't get up there, you've got to admit it's pretty cool to have an old European-style tower on our campus, right? Bet Allbright's doesn't have one!"

The others laughed and agreed. Then Malory stepped to the doorway to check on the ponies.

"Uh oh," she said. "Tybalt looks kind of tense. Maybe we should go."

Dylan looked out over her shoulder. While the other three ponies were still grazing contentedly, Tybalt had danced to the end of his lead rope and was straining against it, staring bug-eyed at every bird flitting past or squirrel rustling in the leaves.

"Yeah," she agreed, sorry that the ride was almost over but very glad that they'd finally fit it in. "It's probably time to head back anyway if we don't want to miss dinner."

Chapter Four

"My brain hurts," Dylan moaned as she and her friends hurried down the path to the stableyard. "I hope Aunt Ali doesn't work us too hard today."

Malory shot her a look. "You're out of luck. We don't have Ms Carmichael for riding class today, remember? We have Mr Musgrave for dressage."

That made Dylan groan again. Mr Musgrave was the stern ex-military man who taught equitation and dressage to the Chestnut Hill riders. He was a knowledgeable, talented instructor, but also a tough one who didn't accept any excuse for a student not trying her hardest. And after a full Monday of classes, with teachers who seemed determined to outdo one another in piling on the challenging assignments, Dylan wasn't sure she was ready for one of Mr Musgrave's lessons!

"I know how you feel, Dyl," Lani said as the girls rounded the corner of the barn. "I can't believe Ms Griffiths wants us to read five chapters of *Pride and Prejudice* by the end of the weekend."

Honey nodded. "It's as if the teachers are trying to

remind us that eighth grade is supposed to be a lot harder than seventh."

"They already did that at the beginning of the semester," Malory said with a sigh. "I wish they'd get over it already. They're going to wear us out so we're too tired to do any decent riding!"

"No way," Lani said immediately. "We'll never be too tired for that. Right, guys?"

"I'm not so sure," Dylan said. "If Mrs O'Hara gives us one more pop math quiz, I might just have to scream. And that would probably annoy her enough to make her give us *another* quiz."

Still, she couldn't help perking up as soon as she set foot in the barn. Breathing in the pleasant scents of horses and hay, she hurried to Morello's stall. He was hanging out over his half-door, blinking sleepily at her.

"Ready to go?" she said as she let herself into the stall. "I hope you'll take it easy on me – I've had a rough day."

A few minutes later Morello was tacked up and Dylan was mounted and warming up along the rail of the indoor arena along with the rest of the eighth-grade intermediate riding class. Morello was feeling sluggish, and Dylan found herself working much harder than usual to get him going.

She'd finally managed a decent circuit at trot when Mr Musgrave strode to the centre, tapping his tall boots with the end of a crop. "Line up and face me, please," he commanded.

Dylan put her right leg just behind the girth to help turn Morello toward the centre of the ring. Instead of moving away from the pressure, the pony put his ears back, swished his tail, and humped his back.

"Quit!" Dylan growled, giving him a sharp kick. "Come on, boy. Stop being cranky!" She could tell it was one of the pony's moody, uncooperative days. Such days were rare but not unheard of; normally Dylan took them as a challenge, but today she wished she could trade him in for the more usual Morello – the high-spirited but reliable one.

They were the last pair to line up, taking a spot at the end of the line next to Lynsey on her own pony, Bluegrass. Mr Musgrave waited, staring at Dylan until Morello came to a more-or-less square halt.

"All right then," the instructor said at last, surveying the group. "I can see that we've all been getting sloppy in some of our basics lately."

Dylan winced. Had Mr Musgrave glanced at her on the word "sloppy"?

"Therefore, we're going to spend some time today polishing up our transitions." The instructor paced in front of the line of ponies as he spoke. "I want you all to begin by tracking left at medium walk. I shall then start calling out gaits at random intervals. I will expect you and your mount to respond promptly with a clean transition. Halts should be immediate, smooth and square. Walk and trot should show impulsion – no lolly-gagging about. Running into the canter from a trot shall not be tolerated. Downward transitions should show a continuation of forward thinking and preparation for the next upward transition. Do we understand?"

Dylan nodded along with the others, not daring to emit the groan she felt coming at Mr Musgrave's instructions. She and Morello were pretty good at transitions – usually. Today, she had a feeling it might be a different story.

Sure enough, by the end of the lesson her legs and back were aching. Morello had remained stubborn and lazy throughout much of the hour, though he'd improved after a while and by the end was approaching his normal forward-thinking self. Mr Musgrave had even made a point of praising the pony's final halt-canter transition, though noting in the same breath that Dylan's position could be better.

"Ugh," she said to her friends as they all converged in the tack room a few minutes later to wipe down and put away their saddles and bridles. "It was bad enough that my brain was like jelly after the rest of the day. Now my legs are like jelly, too!"

Honey shot her a sympathetic look as she ran a rag over Minnie's French link snaffle. "I hear you. Still, I'd rather work way too hard in riding class than in any other class of the day, even if I do ache for hours after."

That was just like Honey – looking on the bright side whenever possible. Still, Dylan had to admit she had a point.

"Let's hurry and finish up here," she said. "Last one back to Adams is a rotten egg!"

"Is that their minibus?" Lani shaded her eyes against the bright afternoon sunshine. Though the days were growing cooler all the time as October neared its end, the sun seemed determined to make up for it by shining more brightly than ever, making it seem like the sunset-hued leaves clinging to the oaks, maples and sweetgums were glowing from within.

Dylan glanced up from fastening Tiptoe's throatlatch. "That's it," she confirmed as she saw the white Cheney Manor bus pulling into the parking area.

Five of the Chestnut Hill ponies were tacked up and waiting in the stable yard with a volunteer leader at each head; once again Dylan had commandeered Tiptoe. The seventh-graders were in the middle of their Wednesday afternoon riding class with jumping instructor Aiden Phillips, which meant Dylan and her friends had been called into service this time along with ninth-grader Olivia Buckley. Predictably, Lynsey had been nowhere in sight when the call for help went out.

The ongoing riding lesson also meant that several of the usual ponies were unavailable, so sweet, calm Minnie had been called into service with Dylan and Honey's permission. Honey was leading her, of course. Malory was standing with Tudor and Lani with Blaze, leaving Olivia with Bella.

Ms Carmichael went over to meet the minibus. She had told her volunteer helpers that only five kids would be coming to ride that day, though Dylan hadn't had a chance to ask which ones. She hoped Casey would be among them – after their difficult start the previous weekend, she'd ended up really liking the prickly but bright younger girl.

She and her friends drifted closer as the van door opened. Howard was the first one out again.

"Yee-haw!" he yelled at the top of his lungs, making even lazy Bella's ears prick forward. "Let's ride, cowboys!"

"That's Howard," Dylan told the others. "He's very enthusiastic."

Honey smiled. "So I see," she said. "Er, rather, so I *hear*."

The rest of the kids piled out. Dylan was pleased to see that Casey was among them. Casey's eyes almost immediately zeroed in on Tiptoe, and a huge smile transformed her face.

"Is that Casey?" Malory guessed.

"Uh huh." Dylan tugged gently on Tiptoe's reins to get her moving. Then she made her way over to the younger girl. "Hi," she said, lifting one hand in what she hoped was an appropriate sign-language greeting.

Casey lifted a hand in return. That huge smile had disappeared, though her hazel eyes were soft as she looked at Tiptoe and raised a hand to stroke her soft nose.

Jill, the woman who had translated during the previous lesson, hurried towards them from the minibus. "Well, hello, Dylan," she said. "Will you be leading for us again?"

"Yep," Dylan confirmed. "I'm really glad you guys came back."

Jill translated what Dylan had said for Casey, who ducked her head shyly and shot Dylan a tiny smile before returning her attention to Tiptoe. Dylan was pleased. They were off to a much better start already!

Soon the Cheney Manor kids were mounted and being led around the outdoor ring. Once again, Ms Carmichael directed them to take a few moments getting used to the feel of their mounts and also allowing the ponies to warm up.

"Did you translate that part for her?" Dylan asked with a glance at Jill. "About the warming up, I mean."

Jill nodded. Dylan turned to look directly at Casey when she spoke next, recalling the misunderstanding from last time.

"Tiptoe likes a good warm-up even more than most ponies," she said. "She's older and has jumped a lot in her life, so she can be a little stiff at first. But you can tell when she's ready to go by watching her neck. She'll start out with it kind of stretched out and flat, like it is now." She ran a hand along Tiptoe's crest. "But once she's feeling looser, her topline will sort of round out as she starts to carry herself properly."

"That's interesting, Dylan," Jill said after she'd translated Dylan's comments for Casey, still moving her hands to translate her own words as she went along. "I suppose since horses can't communicate with us verbally, it helps to know their body language. Are there other things to watch for?"

"Tons," Dylan said, speaking to both Jill and Casey now. "For instance, you can learn a lot about your pony's mood by watching his or her ears. See how Tiptoe is pricking her ears forward? That means she's

interested and paying attention to where she's going."
She turned and pointed to the pony Howard was riding.
"Meanwhile Blaze's ears are floppy, see? That shows that
he's feeling lazy. But that's no surprise – Blaze is almost
always feeling lazy."

She paused to give Jill a chance to translate. At the
end, she was surprised when Casey let out a giggle.
Dylan grinned, glad that she had appreciated her joke

"And then there's Minnie." Dylan pointed out the
pretty grey pony who was walking obediently beside
Honey with Charisse on her back. "She has one ear
cocked back and one forward. Minnie is very well
trained and that cocked-back ear shows that she's
paying attention to her rider."

She gave Casey and Jill a few more tips about
equine body language before Ms Carmichael called for
attention. "All right, we're going to start the lesson today
by reviewing what we learned last time."

"When do we get to gallop?" Howard shouted,
dropping his reins and pumping both small fists over his
head. "I wanna be a cowboy. Yee-haw!"

"Hush up, Howard!" Charisse complained. "I don't
want to gallop!"

Lani, who was Howard's leader, let out a laugh.
"Don't worry," she said. "I don't think most of these
ponies are going to gallop unless they're following a
runaway carrot."

Charisse let out a shout of laughter. "A runaway
carrot?" she exclaimed. "That's crazy!"

Dylan glanced over to make sure Casey was keeping

up. Jill was busy translating for her, and after a moment Casey let out a laugh.

Meanwhile Howard looked disappointed. "But I want to gallop!" he insisted. "Cowboys always gallop!"

"Actually, that's not true," Lani said. "See, I live out west, so I know all about what real cowboys do."

"Really?" Howard stared down at her, looking sceptical.

"Uh huh. See? I've even got cowboy boots." Lani held up one foot. Sure enough, she was wearing her favourite battered Western boots, the ones that made Lynsey sniff and roll her eyes whenever she saw them. "Anyway, I happen to know that cowboys don't gallop unless they have to. See, they rely on their horses for their livelihood. So they take really good care of them and don't ask them to go fast unless it's necessary."

"Really?" Howard said again, though this time he seemed much more convinced that Lani might actually know what she was talking about.

Dylan grinned as she listened along with the rest of the class. *See?* she thought. *You never know when Lani's Wild West background is going to come in handy!*

Lani nodded solemnly. "Really, pardner," she said. "So I know you'll want to take good care of Blaze here and not push him too hard. Because I can see you're a true cowboy at heart."

"I am!" Howard puffed out his chest. "So let's giddy-up, pardners! And we don't have to gallop unless, um…" He glanced at Lani again for help.

"Well, maybe if a runaway steer runs past," Lani said. "Then we might have to gallop."

"What about a runaway carrot?" Charisse called out.

"Sure," Lani agreed. "If a runaway steer or a runaway carrot happens by, we might have to gallop after them. Otherwise, maybe we'll just stick to walk and trot for today."

"That's right," Ms Carmichael said, clearly holding back a smile. "Now that that's settled, let's get started on some walk to halt to walk transitions..."

Just then Dylan heard Casey speak up, though her words were too garbled to make out. She glanced back at the younger girl. "Um, sorry," she said, feeling uncomfortable. "I didn't catch that. I'm sorry."

"It's all right, Dylan." Jill smiled at her. "Casey's been working hard on her speech, but if you're not used to listening to her it's still quite difficult to follow." She sighed and glanced at the girl. "It's too bad – if only we could find a set of hearing aids that suit her, she would have a much easier time making herself understood verbally. I think it would really help her fit in with the other kids, and give her more confidence in general."

"Oh." Dylan was surprised to hear the woman mention hearing aids. She'd assumed that deaf meant deaf – that Casey would never be able to hear anything at all. "Still, I wish I could understand her better. I feel kind of stupid not being able to communicate with her, you know?"

"Don't feel that way," Jill said. "But if it helps, we could teach you a few more signs."

Dylan nodded immediately. "That would be great!" she said. "Lay them on me."

Jill turned and consulted with Casey for a moment in ASL. Then she glanced back at Dylan.

"I just asked Casey which signs we should teach you," she reported. "She says we should start with the most important ones – like the ones for 'horse', 'ride' and 'stable'."

Dylan grinned and glanced at Casey. "I like the way you think!" she told her. As Jill translated, Casey smiled shyly back at Dylan.

By the end of the lesson, Casey was looking relaxed and comfortable in the saddle, with her heels down and her hands steady on the reins. Along with the rest of the class, she had learned the basics of steering, tried a little more trotting, and even practised adjusting her position as Tiptoe stepped carefully over some ground poles. As for Dylan, she had learned at least half a dozen more signs and was starting to know how to sign the letters of the alphabet.

The Cheney Manor kids were ready to leave after watching the volunteers untack the ponies and put them back in their stalls. As they walked out towards the minibus, Dylan felt confident enough to sign "goodbye" to Casey and Jill.

"Did I get it right?" she asked them.

"You did," Jill confirmed, while Casey smiled and signed "goodbye" in return.

Dylan grinned. "Cool. I'm definitely going to study up on this stuff before you guys come back."

"That's great. It's not too hard to pick up some of the basics," Jill said. "Just check out those ASL websites I mentioned and you should be good to go."

"Thanks," Dylan said. "Maybe by next time we won't even need you to translate!"

Jill chuckled and signed what Dylan had just said. Casey looked sceptical, but shrugged and shot Dylan another quick smile before turning and hurrying towards the bus.

"Thanks, Dylan," Jill said after Casey had disappeared inside the vehicle. "I can tell Casey likes you. She's really starting to come out of her shell."

"Well, Tiptoe probably has more to do with that than I do," Dylan replied modestly, though she couldn't help feeling pleased. "But thanks. She's really cool."

She waved as the bus pulled away. Honey wandered up to stand beside her. "Was that ASL I saw you doing?" she asked.

Dylan nodded. "Casey and Jill are teaching me," she said, giving one last wave before turning back towards the stable with Honey, feeling cheerful and contented with the way the afternoon had gone. "It's cool learning how to talk with my hands – it really is a whole different language. In fact, I wish I could study it full-time instead of stupid old French. For one thing, I'd probably get a much better grade!"

Chapter Five

Dylan crept down the dorm hallway and paused outside a particular door. Clutching her homemade monster mask to her face, she took a deep breath, shoved the door open, and leaped into the darkened room with a loud "Graaaaaawrrrrr!"

She was startled when several large, pale shapes jumped towards her out of the dimness, yelling "Whooooooooooooooo!"

"Hey!" she blurted out, yanking off her mask so she could see better. She blinked as the three ghostly shapes started to giggle. They looked an awful lot like three girls draped in sheets... Sure enough, a second later the tallest of the ghosts pulled off its sheet, revealing a grinning Lani.

"Gotcha!" Lani crowed. She turned to Honey and Malory, who had just removed their sheets as well. "See? I told you Dylan would try to scare us this morning."

Honey shook her head. "Seems I was the naive one," she said. "Here I thought she might wait till lunchtime at least."

Dylan grinned sheepishly. "Happy Halloween," she said, tossing her mask on to Honey's bed. It was Thursday morning, which meant it was Halloween – Dylan's favourite holiday. She had been determined to catch her friends off guard by starting the spooky fun early. Instead, it seemed they had been the ones to catch her!

A few minutes later they were stepping into the dining hall. Normally breakfast was a fairly sedate meal, with girls yawning over their cereal and toast and sucking down great quantities of coffee, tea or fruit juice to help them wake up. Today, however, there seemed to be more than the usual number of squeals and shouts of laughter coming from inside the cafeteria.

"What's going on in there?" Malory wondered.

"Must be something spoooooky," Dylan intoned, waggling her fingers in Malory's face. "Come on, let's go check it out."

When they joined the cafeteria line, they saw what all the commotion was about. The school's catering staff had entered into the spirit of the holiday, and the usual printed cards reading Scrambled Eggs, Bagels, Grits and so forth had disappeared, to be replaced with garish orange and black signs draped with fake cobwebs.

"Ooh, look," Honey said, pointing to one of the new cards with a shudder and a laugh. "Oatmeal with bloody eyeballs – how horrible!"

Malory leaned over to peer into the tub on the other side of the plastic sneeze guard. "Hmm. Looks like regular oatmeal with cherries in it to me."

"Check it out." Dylan had moved on ahead to check out the other signs. "Ghost Toast! I love it!" She grabbed a slice of the toast, which was cut into the shape of a ghostly figure.

The fun continued after breakfast as well. Most of the teachers had changed their lessons to incorporate a holiday touch. For instance, the girls' maths class was spent calculating the weights and costs of pumpkins, while art class involved creating Halloween-inspired abstract images. Just about the only teacher who didn't seem willing to enter into the spirit of things was Madame Dubois, the dour French teacher.

"That's no surprise," Dylan murmured to Malory once she'd realized that today's lesson was going to be just like every other day's lesson – in other words, boring. "Mme Dubois hates anything fun."

"Ssh," Malory warned, casting an anxious glance at the teacher, who was handing out a worksheet. "If you're going to insult her, at least do it *en français*. You know she hates catching us speaking English!"

Later that day, the girls arrived for their afternoon riding lesson to find Ms Carmichael standing in the middle of the jumping ring wearing a rubber Godzilla mask. She just stood and watched with her arms crossed over her chest as the girls led their ponies in and mounted.

"Nice mask, Ms Carmichael," Dylan said, riding Morello closer for a better look. "Very scary. Aren't you afraid it's going to spook the ponies?"

"Shorten your reins, Dylan," her aunt responded

without acknowledging the comment. "This isn't a Western Pleasure class."

Dylan quickly adjusted her reins to the proper length. "Sorry, Ms Godzilla," she joked.

Ms Carmichael merely turned away to help Tessa Harding with a twisted stirrup, but Dylan was pretty sure she saw a twinkle in the eyes behind the mask's eyeholes. She grinned. Only Aunt Ali could teach a lesson in a monster mask while keeping a straight face. In fact, only she would even think of it!

Guess that trait runs in the family, she thought as she set Morello into a brisk trot along the rail. Fortunately the pony was in a better mood than he'd been in for Monday's class. He seemed energetic and ready to work.

"All right, everyone," Ms. Carmichael said a few minutes later once the girls had warmed up, her voice only slightly muffled by the rubber mask. "As most of you already know, the combination at our mini event last month gave some of you a bit of trouble."

Dylan glanced at Lani, who grimaced. The girls and their ponies had all had fun learning about eventing and competing at Chestnut Hill's first-ever one-day event, which had inaugurated the school's new cross-country course. However, some of the ponies had had a little *too* much fun, including Colorado, who was great at cross country but had gotten too quick in stadium jumping.

"Therefore, we're going to school some combinations today," the instructor went on, stepping towards the set of three fences set down the centre line. The first two were verticals, while the third was an oxer. "You can see that we're keeping the heights fairly low – nothing over 2 foot 3 for now."

"What's the point of practising over such tiny fences?" Lynsey spoke up with obvious disdain. "Blue will probably trip over them, since he won't even notice they're there."

"I doubt that will be a problem, Lynsey," Ms Carmichael said calmly. "And to answer your question, we're keeping things low to save wear and tear on our ponies' legs. The point of the exercise isn't to test their scope; it's to sharpen your eyes and help you learn to adjust their strides more accurately."

Dylan nodded. As much fun as it was to jump bigger fences, she understood that it wasn't good for the ponies to do it too often. Besides, some of the riders in the class, including Honey and Paris Mackenzie, weren't that comfortable jumping anything much over three feet yet.

However, Lynsey seemed less impressed with the answer. "Still, you'd think we could do a little better than beginner-type heights," she commented.

Dylan rolled her eyes at Lani. "You'd think Lynsey was the only one who ever rode in an A show, the way she keeps mentioning it every chance she gets," she muttered.

Lani snorted. "Tell me about it."

But there wasn't much time to worry over Lynsey's snooty behaviour. Soon all eight students in the class were hard at work over the grid. Even though the jumps were low, the striding was tight and rather tricky. The first time through, Colorado went too fast and left out a stride before the oxer. Lani barely hung on as the agile buckskin put in an awkward half-stride and leaped up from an extra-close distance, twisting his body to get over and bringing the front rail down with his forelegs.

"You'll have to hold him together more firmly, Lani," Ms Carmichael called as she hurried forward to replace the rail. "I know he can cover a lot of ground – he's got a horse-sized stride in a pony-sized package. But it's your job to help him collect or extend as necessary to fit that stride into the grid."

Lani nodded, red-faced and breathless. "Right," she said. "We'll get it next time." She reached down to pat Colorado, who was blowing and seemed agitated after the clumsy jump.

Lynsey glanced over at Paris, who was sitting beside her on her own mare, Whisper. "It's pretty obvious who's used to handling a real show-jumping course on a real jumper and who's used to yee-hawing across the range on some fat old stock horse," she said in a loud stage whisper.

"Lynsey? Did I hear you volunteering to go next?" Ms Carmichael asked from behind her mask. "Let's see you and Blue give it a try."

"No problem." Lynsey took up the slack in her reins and set Bluegrass into motion. The experienced show pony settled immediately into a steady canter, moving like clockwork in a neat circle before Lynsey turned to aim him at the combination. He tucked his dark hooves neatly at each fence, easily fitting in the correct number of strides between each one.

"Very good," Ms Carmichael said when the pair had finished. "That's exactly what we're aiming for here. Malory? Ready to give it a try?"

"Sure," Malory said, nudging Tybalt forward.

Dylan held her breath. *Poor Mal!* she thought. *It's got to be hard enough to finesse Tybalt through an exercise like this, let alone having to follow Miss Perfect and her Perfect Performing Pony!*

As it turned out, she needn't have worried. Tybalt pricked his ears at the first element and started to surge forward. But Malory kept him in hand, talking to him in a low, soothing voice as she tactfully compressed his stride. They met the first fence perfectly, arcing up and over as prettily as Bluegrass had just done. The second and third elements went just as well, and by the time she pulled up Malory was grinning from ear to ear.

"Excellent, Malory!" Ms Carmichael said. "Tybalt is really jumping well today."

"He is, isn't he?" Malory beamed and rubbed the bay gelding on his withers. "I think he's glad to be feeling better again after the Lyme and everything."

After sending everyone through the combination a second time, Ms Carmichael started switching things around to create different challenges. First she set the oxer in the middle of two verticals, then built a second oxer for the last element. She even raised the fences a few inches towards the end, though still not high enough for Lynsey's taste.

Still, they were high enough that Minnie appeared to be struggling to get over them, and wound up taking down a rail on the last vertical. "Sorry," Honey said breathlessly as she pulled up and gave the mare a pat. "I'm probably messing her up or something. I'm sure my timing isn't as good as it could be."

"It's all right, Honey," Ms Carmichael said. "Why don't you both sit out the next round? Minnie does look a bit tired, and there's no sense in pushing these ponies to their limits."

So there, A-Circuit Snoberella, Dylan thought, wondering if her aunt had meant the comment as much for Lynsey as for Honey.

After the lesson, Dylan found her friends in the tack room. "So I've been thinking about the party tonight," she said, referring to the Halloween celebration being held at their dorm that evening. "Since I didn't come out shopping with you guys last weekend, I still don't have a costume. What do you think of me wearing my show clothes and going as a show jumper or something?" She grinned. "In fact, if we can get our hands on a long blonde wig and some overpriced glitter make-up, I could go as Lynsey the A-Circuit Princess."

Lani laughed, but Honey and Malory exchanged a look and shook their heads. "We have a better idea, Dylan," Honey spoke up.

"Yeah," Malory added. "Don't worry about a costume. We've got it covered."

It didn't take much to pique Dylan's curiosity, and

it was definitely piqued now. "What do you mean?" she demanded. "What are you guys not telling me?"

"Patience, grasshopper." Lani slung an arm around her shoulders and steered her out of the barn. "All will become clear in time."

"In time" turned out to translate roughly to "right after dinner". That was when Dylan's friends dragged her into Lani and Honey's room and revealed their secret: a fake set of jockey's silks. The royal-blue-and-silver checked shirt and matching cap were laid out on Lani's bed.

"Oh my gosh!" Dylan shrieked, grabbing the shirt and holding it up for a better look. "This is perfect! It's for me?"

Honey nodded. "We got it last weekend in town," she said. "The boys helped us pick it out."

"Yeah," Malory added. "For some reason all the guys thought this would suit you perfectly."

Lani laughed. "I guess they've heard about how you ride, Walsh – full speed ahead!"

"Anyway, we thought you could wear it with your white breeches and your show boots and carry a crop," Malory said. "And see? We even found something pretty close to Chestnut Hill's school colours!"

"It's kind of chintzy fabric, and it's actually supposed to be a little kid's costume, but we figured you're petite enough to fit in the extra large," Honey explained.

Dylan slipped the shirt on over what she was wearing to check. "Perfect!" she declared, holding the front together and turning from side to side in front of the mirror over Honey's dresser. "This is so awesome! I thought I might be stuck wearing that monster mask I made out of cardboard and a green sweatshirt." She grinned, thinking back to that afternoon's riding class. "Or maybe borrowing Aunt Ali's Godzilla mask," she added.

"That was pretty funny." Malory shook her head with a smile. "I thought Tybalt was going to come out of his skin when he first walked in and saw her."

"Oh, I didn't even think about that!" Honey exclaimed.

"Yeah, Morello doesn't spook at weird stuff like that." Dylan slipped off the jockey's shirt and rolled her eyes. "But leave a manure fork in the aisle, and look out!"

Malory laughed along with the others. "Tyb settled down pretty quickly once he heard Ms Carmichael's voice coming out of the mask. I guess he figured it wasn't too smart to be scared of the person who feeds him, no matter what she looks like."

Meanwhile Lani was digging into a shopping bag at the foot of her bed. She straightened up holding a skeleton costume. "Come on, let's get dressed," she said. "The party starts in half an hour!"

Exactly half an hour later, Dylan and her friends were walking into the dorm lobby, where the party was being held. Someone had clearly been working hard on decorating and the place was dripping with fake cobwebs and spiders, cutouts of ghosts and goblins, and lighted jack o'lanterns flickering everywhere. Spooky sound effects were playing on someone's iPod and speakers. A buffet table had been set up near the staircase and was well stocked with punchbowls and plates of cookies, cupcakes and other treats.

Most of the dorm's residents had already arrived and were milling around exclaiming over one another's costumes. A few people were showing off fancy costumes that had obviously been quite expensive, like freshman Kathryn MacIntyre, who was wearing some sort of lush Renaissance-style gown and had her long black hair piled so elaborately on top of her head that it had to have been done specially at the hairdresser's. But most Adams residents had chosen to get creative with cheaper or homemade outfits. For instance, Deborah Smith was wearing a beautiful set of salwar kameez and dupatta that had presumably been borrowed from her Pakistani roommate, Aggninder Dillon, while Aggninder herself had dressed up as a cloud by attaching hundreds of cotton wool balls to an old blue sweatshirt.

"This is amazing!" Honey gasped, looking adorable in her fluffy puppy costume. Beside her, Malory was dressed as a vampire, and Lani looked great in her skeleton outfit.

Dylan was pleased with the way her jockey's outfit had turned out. Even though the shirt and cap weren't expensive or even particularly authentic, they really looked the part once paired with her own riding gear.

"Come on, let's go try the punch," she suggested.

They were halfway to the snack table when someone else started down the steps. "Whoa, check out Lynsey's outfit!" Razina called out, pointing.

Dylan glanced up and saw Lynsey coming down one side of the ornate, curving double staircase. She was dressed in a head-to-toe skintight black Lycra catsuit that twinkled with black Swarovski crystals. A long, twitching tail floated out behind her and pointy little black ears sat atop her sleek blonde hair.

"Check out the whiskers," Lani commented. "It looks like they actually light up!"

As more people turned to stare, Lynsey paused on the staircase and posed like some kind of Hollywood starlet. Then she came down a few more steps and paused again, turning slightly so that everyone could admire her from a different angle.

"Where does she think she is, the Academy Awards of Halloween costumes?" Dylan said with a snort.

She'd meant it for her friends' ears only. Unfortunately, the spooky sounds faded out at that moment, allowing her words to ring out clearly for all to hear – including Lynsey.

Lynsey looked down at her and smirked. "Jealous much, Dylan?" she said smugly, continuing down the steps.

"As if," Dylan retorted. "Why would I be jealous of someone who isn't even creative enough to come up with her own costume, and just buys something flashy to cover up her own inadequacy?"

Lynsey flicked an invisible bit of lint off her hipbone, seeming unperturbed by the insult. "If you must know, I didn't just go out and buy it. My mother had it made to order for me by her favourite boutique in New York. I'd tell you which one, but judging by the way you dress I seriously doubt you've ever heard of it." She allowed her supercilious gaze to wander down Dylan's outfit.

"It's very nice, Lynsey," Malory spoke up quickly, putting a hand on Dylan's arm as if to steer her away. "Come on, Dyl. Let's—"

"What's your problem, Lynsey?" Dylan blurted out, too fed up with Lynsey's attitude to hold her tongue this time. "Why are you always trying to show everyone up all the time? It's pathetic!"

Lynsey shrugged. "I just like to be the best, that's all," she replied coolly. "I wouldn't expect someone like you to relate to *that*."

Dylan gritted her teeth. "Oh yeah?" she shot back. "How come I had a faster time than yours in the fifty-yard dash in gym class last week? And why does Lani kick your butt on every maths test?"

"Hey, leave me out of this," Lani protested.

Lynsey had reached the bottom step by now. She put her hands on her Lycra-covered hips. "Grow up, Dylan," she said icily. "Life isn't a contest, you know. Which is just as well, for you. If it was, you'd lose."

Patience had hurried over just in time to hear her friend's last comment. "Good one, Lyns!" she said with a laugh. "And hey, you look super hot!"

"Thanks." Lynsey cast a cursory glance over Patience's outfit. She was dressed in a pink, black and white designer gown. "You too."

"Thanks." Patience shot a smug look at Dylan and her friends. "I got the idea from Lynsey's fabulous idea for the Christmas fundraiser. Too bad everyone else couldn't appreciate a classy idea when they heard it."

"Right. Come on, Dylan," Lani said. "Let's go get that punch now."

But Dylan wasn't ready to let Lynsey have the last word. "That idea was lame, and you know it," she snapped. "Who ever heard of a pink-and-black Christmas? It's totally stupid!"

Lynsey frowned. "Just you wait," she said. "Patience and I are going to make some really tasteful French-style ornaments with crystals and beads and pink ribbons. I bet they outsell whatever clothespin-and-button piece of junk you come up with."

"Oh really?" Dylan crossed her arms over her chest. "How much do you want to bet?"

Lynsey rolled her eyes. "Don't be ridiculous."

"No, I'm serious," Dylan insisted. "If you're so confident, put your money where your mouth is!"

"Come on, Dylan," Honey said soothingly. "Wouldn't you rather donate your money to Cheney Manor rather than betting it with Lynsey?"

"Hmm, good point." Dylan thought for a second. "I have a better idea." She pointed her crop at Lynsey. "If your stupid classy crystal whatevers raise more money for Cheney Manor than whatever my friends and I do, I'll, um, get rid of my night light."

Lynsey cocked an eyebrow. "I'm listening," she said.

"And if we raise more money with our stuff, you have to let the Cheney Manor kids ride Blue next time they come for a riding lesson."

"What?" Lynsey shrieked, finally losing her cool. "You're nuts. I'm not letting some stupid orphan ride Blue!"

"Oh, but if you're so sure you'll win, what's the problem?" Dylan taunted. "Maybe you're not so confident about those silly French decorations after all, hmm?"

Lynsey scowled. "Fine. You're right – there's no way I'll lose. Not with a much better product plus all those years observing my mother's fundraising skills. You're on!"

"Lynsey, are you sure?" Patience exclaimed.

At the same time, Malory said, "Dylan, wait..."

But they were too late. Dylan grabbed Lynsey's hand and shook it firmly. "It's a bet."

Chapter Six

Dylan stepped to the end of the barn aisle to peer outside. It was Saturday, and she'd purposely put Tiptoe in the endmost set of cross-ties so she could keep an eye out for the Cheney Manor minibus while tacking her up. Five additional ponies were lined up at the other ties or being groomed and tacked in their stalls. Several more ponies and horses, including Morello, were watching the hubbub curiously over their half-doors. The seventh-graders had taken over most of the leading duties again. Honey was going out to lunch with her family and Malory had a geography essay due on Monday, so they had begged off this time and only Lani had accompanied Dylan down to the yard to help out.

"They're here!" Dylan cried as she spotted the vehicle heading up the drive. She hurried back just long enough to give Tiptoe a pat. "Be good, girl," she whispered. "I'll be right back." Then she raised her voice to a normal level. "Hey, Joanna, can you keep an eye on the T-girl for a sec?"

She hardly waited for the other girl's "sure" before

rushing outside. She was waiting, hopping impatiently from foot to foot, when Jill got out of the passenger side of the van and stepped back to open the side door.

"Oh, hello, Dylan," the woman said. "Nice to see you again."

"Yeah, you too. Did Casey come?"

Jill nodded. "She wouldn't miss it."

She opened the door, and as usual Howard burst out. "Time to ride the range! Yee-haw!"

Dylan grinned as he raced towards the barn with one of the other adults chasing after him. Then she returned her attention to the kids jumping out of the bus. Charisse was there again, along with Brittany and two others. Finally Casey poked her head out and looked around.

"Hi, Casey!" Dylan said.

Jill touched the girl on the arm and gestured towards Dylan. Casey glanced her way and ducked her head forward so her brown hair fell over most of her face.

Still, Dylan figured she could probably see her well enough. "Welcome," she said aloud, simultaneously signing the words she'd taught herself from some ASL websites. "I'm glad you're here. Tiptoe is glad, too."

She had to spell out Tiptoe's name letter by letter, which took a little while, especially since she forgot for a moment how to form the letter P. But she was pretty sure she'd gotten most of it right. When she finished, she grinned at Casey.

"Very good, Dylan!" Jill said. "I can see you've been studying."

"Thanks," Dylan said, signing the word. "ASL is fun!"

She wasn't sure how to sign that, so she just waited for Jill to translate for her.

"Casey, could you hear what Dylan just said?" Jill asked the girl instead.

Dylan blinked. "Huh?"

Jill chuckled. "Oh, sorry, Dylan," she said. "I was just about to tell you – Casey was fitted for new hearing aids yesterday. She's wearing them now."

"Really?" Dylan looked at Casey, who was staring at the ground with her hair still hanging over her face. Her hair also completely covered her ears. "Does that mean you can hear me, Casey?"

Casey glanced up just long enough to show that she had. Then she shrugged and mumbled something while making a quick sign.

Jill frowned. "Oh, Casey…" She sighed and glanced at Dylan. "She said the hearing aids are uncomfortable."

Before Dylan could respond, one of the other Cheney Manor adults came outside. "Is Casey ready?" the woman asked. "Ms Carmichael is about to give a quick demonstration about grooming. Come along, dear – you'll enjoy this now that you can hear it, mmm?" She grabbed Casey by the hand and dragged her off.

Once they'd disappeared into the barn, Jill sighed again and shook her head. "I'm afraid Casey is a bit self-conscious about wearing her hearing aids."

"What do you mean?" Dylan was surprised. "I mean, I can see that hearing aids aren't exactly the hip, happening accessory that every girl wants to complete their outfit. But come on – anything's better than being deaf, right?"

"Not exactly," Jill said gently. "See, Casey has always been deaf. It's what she's used to, and she copes well in her world."

"Oh." Dylan had never thought about it that way before. "But still..."

"It's easy for the hearing world to see people like Casey as lacking something," Jill went on, glancing towards the barn with a frown. "But the thing is, she's a complete person even though she doesn't hear. She has a regular life, friends, interests, fears, passions. Just like you and your classmates."

"Yeah," Dylan said. "I guess I wasn't looking at it like that. It would be really hard to make such a major, sudden change. Even if it's for the better."

"Right. On the other hand, it *is* important that Casey accept and get accustomed to her hearing aids. It will help her speech become more intelligible, and will also enable her to expand her world." She cast another worried glance towards the barn. "Come on, we'd better get inside."

Dylan nodded and followed her, thinking hard about what she'd just learned. *I always took hearing for granted*, she thought. *But if being deaf is all Casey has ever known, it's probably kind of scary to suddenly start hearing stuff.*

It was a weird thought. But definitely one worth pondering further – later. Right now she had a pony to finish getting ready.

After the first ten minutes of the lesson, Ms Carmichael asked the leaders to stay by the ponies' heads but not touch them unless their rider was in trouble. "That way, you guys will be able to really start riding on your own," she told the kids after stopping them in the centre of the ring.

"Yee-haw!" Howard cheered. "When can we be in the rodeo?"

"Sorry, rodeo season's over for the year," Lani told him, straight-faced. "You'll have to wait until next summer."

"Aw, man!" Howard complained.

"Think of it this way, dude," Lani told him. "This means you'll have tons of time to practise so you'll be able to win all the prizes. They give out really cool stuff at the rodeo, you know."

"Oh, yeah!" Howard brightened again immediately. "Cool!"

Dylan grinned as several others, including Ms Carmichael, laughed. "Right," she said. "And one of our rodeo skills is asking the ponies to go from a halt to a walk and then steering them so they go the way we want them to go."

"But I don't want to be in the rodeo!" Charisse called out, sounding anxious.

"Don't worry," Dylan said to her. "This stuff works for regular non-rodeo riding, too."

"Right." Ms Carmichael winked at Dylan. "All right, kids. Let's give it a try – ask your ponies for a walk, then steer them over to the rail and go left. Remember to leave some room between your pony and the one in front of you."

Dylan glanced over at Tiptoe's head, waiting for the

pony to start walking. Casey had already showed at the previous lessons that she understood how to squeeze with her calves to ask the pony to move forward, and Tiptoe was more obedient and willing than some of the lazier ponies and always moved promptly off the leg. So Dylan was surprised when the little mare just stood there.

She turned to check on Casey, wondering if her hearing aids were giving her trouble. It turned out that they were, but not in the way Dylan had thought. The younger girl was sitting slumped in the saddle, her reins dropped on Tiptoe's withers as she fiddled with her left hearing aid with both hands. In the process, she'd knocked her helmet askew.

"Hey, Casey," Dylan said, reaching out and touching her on the knee. "You OK?"

Casey jumped, then nodded. "Fine," she said.

Dylan grinned. "Hey, your speech really is getting better!" she exclaimed. "Good job!"

Casey didn't answer. She quickly shoved her helmet back in place, then let her hair fall over her face as she looked down and gathered up the reins.

Dylan bit her lip and shot a glance towards Jill, who was watching along with the other two Cheney Manor employees from the side of the ring. Jill just shrugged. Then Tiptoe started ambling toward the rail, and Dylan had to scoot forward to keep up.

"All right, today we're going to try something new," Ms Carmichael said when the kids had dismounted at the end of the ride. "Being around horses isn't just about riding. It's important for you to learn how to take care of your ponies, too. We're going to start by having you guys help take off their saddles and bridles and brush them off, OK?"

"Cool." Brittany looked interested. "Do we get to comb their manes and tails?"

"Yes, if you like," Ms. Carmichael said. "Now as we take the ponies over to the rail, I want each of you to walk beside your pony's leader and watch how she leads the pony."

Dylan had been standing with Tiptoe's reins loosely looped over one wrist. Suddenly realizing that she wasn't setting a very good example for the newbies, she stepped over beside the pony's neck and took the reins in both hands in the proper way. Then she looked around for Casey. She was facing away from the pony and the rest of the group. Her helmet was off and sitting on the ground at her feet, and she was pulling her hair forward over her ears.

"Hey, Casey," Dylan said. "Heads up! Let's go find a good spot on the rail, OK?"

Casey peered around at her. Dylan wasn't sure how clearly she could hear even with her hearing aids, so she pantomimed leading Tiptoe towards the rail. Casey just stared at her for a second and Dylan thought about calling Jill over for help. But when she glanced towards where the women had been standing, they were nowhere in sight. Besides, just then Casey ducked down, grabbed her helmet off the ground, and marched off towards the rail.

Dylan shrugged and followed, aiming for a free spot near the gate where they wouldn't be too close to any other ponies. One of the Chestnut Hill stablehands, Kelly, was waiting by the rail with the ponies' halters, which she passed out as the pairs approached. Dylan took Tiptoe's halter and thanked Kelly, then stopped the pony with her head facing the rail and flipped the reins back over her neck.

"Want to help take off her bridle?" she asked Casey. "If you can undo the two buckles, I'll show you how to slide it off over her ears and hold on to the reins around her neck so she can't get away."

She smiled at Tiptoe, who showed little inclination for running away. The pony was standing stock-still, blinking sleepily with one hind foot cocked.

Casey had one hand at her ear, but she took a step forward. She glanced at Dylan, then quickly reached out and unbuckled the noseband.

"Great job!" Dylan said. "Don't forget the throatlatch, though."

But Casey had already turned away and started fiddling with her hair and hearing aids again. Dylan wasn't sure whether she'd heard her or not. Glancing over at Lani and Howard, who were a few yards down the rail, she saw that they had Blaze's bridle off and the pony tied up by his halter. Lani was already showing the little boy how to loosen the girth on the saddle. Not wanting to fall too far behind, Dylan undid the throatlatch herself, sliding the bridle off and the halter on.

"Want to watch and see how to tie a quick-release knot?" she asked Casey, who was tugging at her hair. "That's the safest way to tie up a pony."

Casey shrugged, which Dylan decided to take as a yes. She demonstrated the knot, though when she glanced back to see if Casey was following, she couldn't tell if the younger girl was even paying attention. She had both hands at her ears again and was sort of staring into space.

Just then Jill reappeared along with the other two women from Cheney Manor. They were followed by Sarah, the second Chestnut Hill stablehand. All of them were carrying buckets full of grooming tools.

"OK," Ms Carmichael said. "Now that most of you have your saddles off, it's time to learn how to groom your ponies."

"Yikes," Dylan muttered, realizing she was further behind than she'd thought. Not wanting to waste time coaxing Casey into helping, she hurried over and unbuckled the girth, then hauled off Tiptoe's saddle.

I'll show her the ropes next time, she promised herself as she grabbed the pad and slung it over the saddle. *Maybe by then she'll be used to those hearing aids and actually want to pay attention.*

She set the saddle and pad on the rail, then brushed off her hands and glanced over her shoulder. "OK, now comes the fun part," she began, before realizing that Casey wasn't standing where she'd last seen her.

Blinking in surprise, she glanced around. Casey had vanished. She wasn't behind Dylan or at Tiptoe's head or leaning against the rail. Dylan even ducked down to look under the pony's belly to make sure the girl wasn't standing on Tiptoe's other side. But there was no sign of her anywhere.

She looked over at Jill, wondering if Casey had gone over to her. But the woman was busy handing out grooming tools with the others, and Casey wasn't with her. Jill didn't appear to have noticed yet that the girl was missing.

Yikes, Dylan thought with a gulp. *Where could she have gone?*

She stepped away from Tiptoe so she could get a good look at the line of ponies along the rail. Most of the kids were busy with brushes or curries, but Casey was still nowhere in sight.

"Hey, Lani!" Dylan called. "Watch Tiptoe for me, OK? I've got to track down a missing kid."

Lani glanced up from showing Howard how to pick out Blaze's feet, looking surprised, but Dylan didn't stick around for any questions. She ducked between the rails of the ring fence and hurried towards the barn.

Inside, all was still and quiet except for the peaceful sounds of the horses and ponies chewing hay or moving around in their stalls. Dylan opened her mouth to call Casey's name, then shut it again, feeling frustrated. Even with her hearing aids, it was unlikely that Casey would be able to hear her call from more than a few yards away. In any case, it was clear enough that she wasn't in the aisle, so Dylan jogged down to the far end towards the tack room.

"I'm not ignoring you, boy," she called out to Morello as she went past his stall. "I'll have plenty of treats for you later. Right now, I need to find somebody."

Morello was standing halfway back in his stall and barely flicked an ear towards her as she passed. Even in the midst of her worry, Dylan couldn't help a flash of surprise. Usually the friendly pinto was the first one to shove his head out into the aisle, mugging passers-by for treats.

The tack room door was ajar, and a quick glance around the neatly organized interior was all it took to see that Casey wasn't inside. Dylan sighed and leaned against the door frame for a moment, wondering where to look next.

The minibus? she thought. *I doubt anyone bothered to lock it. Maybe Casey's hiding out in there.*

She stepped back into the aisle and glanced back down to the other end. By now most of the barn's residents had noted her arrival and were hanging their heads out over the half doors, staring at her with pricked ears as if in an attempt to hypnotize her into feeding them treats. The only head missing was...

"Morello?" Dylan murmured. There was no sign of the gelding's head poking out with the others. That wasn't like him. Even if he'd been napping when she'd passed his stall before, he would have perked up and come to see what was happening when he heard the other horses start to nicker at her.

For a second her heart clenched with panic as she wondered if he was colicking or something. Or maybe he'd come down with Lyme disease, like Tybalt had. "Oh great, that's all I need right now with Casey missing..." she muttered.

Her words trailed off and her eyes narrowed as another possibility occurred to her. She hurried towards the stall and undid the latch.

"Hey, Morello," she said to the pony, who was still standing stock-still in the middle of his stall. "What's going on? You haven't seen a missing girl by any chance, have you?"

Casey gazed up from where she was crouched in the stall's straw bedding. Her face was red and tear-stained. Her hands were buried in the straw, and as Dylan looked at her she quickly yanked them out and stood up, swiping at her damp cheeks with both palms.

"Hi, Casey," Dylan said. "What are you doing in here?"

Casey squinted at her, then shrugged. She made a few signs, but they weren't ones that Dylan recognized.

"Sorry, I don't understand," she said. "Try saying it out loud instead. Your speech is so good with your hearing aids in that I—"

She cut herself off, suddenly realizing that Casey's brown hair was now tucked behind her ears. There was no sign of anything in either of those ears.

"Wait, where are your hearing aids?" Dylan hadn't actually seen the aids, since Casey had been so careful to hide them under her hair until now. But she had to imagine they were fairly easy to spot. Otherwise the younger girl wouldn't be so self-conscious about wearing them.

Casey stared at her defiantly, her lower lip trembling. After a second her gaze wavered and she shot a quick glance at the straw at her feet before gulping and returning her gaze to Dylan again.

"Oh!" Dylan suddenly realized what Casey must have been doing down there in the straw. "Oh, Casey. Is it really that bad?" Impulsively, she stepped towards the girl and gave her a hug. For a second Casey resisted, her thin body as stiff as a board.

But then she gave in, relaxing into the hug. She mumbled something that Dylan couldn't understand.

After a moment Dylan let her go and pulled back, gazing at her seriously. "I'm sorry, Casey," she said, speaking slowly and carefully. Along with her ASL studies, she'd picked up a few tips on the Internet about speaking to lip readers. "You can't hide your hearing aids in here. But don't worry, we're going to help you."

Casey frowned. Dylan wasn't sure whether she was having trouble understanding her or just didn't like what she'd said. Then the younger girl blurted out a few heated words, making Dylan pretty sure she'd understood, though she couldn't make out what Casey was trying to say.

"Sorry," she said again, bending and digging through the straw until she uncovered both hearing aids. Fortunately they appeared fine other than being a little grubby.

Then she straightened up and gave Morello a pat. The gelding snuffled at her expectantly, but Dylan gently pushed his head away. Treats would have to wait until later.

"Come on," she said, grabbing Casey by the hand so she couldn't take off again. "Let's go back before they start to worry."

When they arrived back at the ring, they found Jill standing beside Tiptoe, looking anxious. She smiled with relief when she saw the pair coming.

"Oh, did you need to take her to the restroom or something?" she called out. "Next time, if you wouldn't mind letting me – oh." She stopped as she noticed Casey's swollen eyes and defiant expression.

Dylan quickly explained what had happened. Then she handed over the hearing aids.

"Oh, Casey." Jill bit her lip and shook her head. "You and I had better go back to the bus to wait for the others. Thanks for your help, Dylan."

"You're welcome." Dylan watched them go, wishing there was more she could do to help. But all she could think of to do was turn away and finish taking care of Tiptoe.

Chapter Seven

"I think I know how she feels, at least sort of," Malory said.

Dylan was sitting cross-legged on her bed picking at a loose thread on her duvet cover. Her friends were gathered around her. She'd just finished telling them about Casey being embarrassed by her new hearing aids and trying to hide them in Morello's stall. Lani had seen some of what had happened for herself, of course. But Dylan had made her wait until they were all together to hear the whole story.

"What do you mean?" Lani asked Malory now. "Your hearing is fine, isn't it?"

"Yeah, but when I was younger I had to wear glasses for a while." Malory leaned back against Lynsey's dresser. "It was horrible. I hated those ugly things with a passion and kept trying to lose or break them every chance I got."

"So what happened?" Dylan prompted.

Malory smiled with a hint of sadness in her eyes. "My mom got me some different frames," she said. "They were really cool and funky. That made wearing glasses a lot more fun, and I didn't mind at all after that. I was almost sorry when the eye doctor said I didn't need them any more."

Dylan had never heard that story before. Malory didn't talk much about her mother, who had died several years earlier.

Meanwhile Honey had just sat up straighter on Dylan's desk chair. "That's it!" she declared. "Perhaps that's how we can help poor Casey."

"What do you mean?" Dylan frowned. "Glasses are one thing, but I doubt they make funky, fashionable hearing aids. Maybe that could a niche market for Gucci or someone…"

"No." Honey laughed. "That's not what I mean. But why not accessorize the hearing aids she has? Maybe we can make wearing them seem like fun, the way Malory's mother did for her glasses. I have a cute silk scarf I could donate to the cause. She could wear it as a headband to hold back her hair and hide the hearing aids at the same time."

"Great idea," Malory agreed. "I have some pretty clip-on earrings I never wear that she could have. Maybe wearing those would make her feel better about her ears, too."

Lani nodded. "And I can kick in that pink baseball cap I have. Pink's not really my colour anyway. It'll look much better on Casey."

"Wow," Dylan said, touched that her friends were so eager to help. "That all sounds great! I bet Casey will love it!" She leaned over and grabbed her BlackBerry off the bedside table. "I'm going to call Jill right now and see if Casey can come back tomorrow."

Sunday after breakfast, Dylan and her friends hurried down to the yard carrying their accessories. Jill had agreed to bring Casey back for a short trail ride, and Dylan had cleared it with Ms Carmichael as well.

While they got the ponies ready, Dylan once again kept a lookout for the minibus. However, this time Jill and Casey arrived in an old-looking hatchback.

"Figured we'd save on fuel by bringing my car instead of the bus," Jill explained as she got out and shook hands with Ms Carmichael.

"Makes sense," Ms Carmichael agreed. Then she smiled at Casey, who was climbing out of the car. "Welcome back, Casey."

Casey smiled briefly, then ducked her head so her hair fell forward just as she'd done before. Dylan traded a look with her friends.

"Hey, Casey," Lani said. "We have some cool stuff for you."

Casey shot her a glance, then looked at the ground. Jill put a hand on the girl's shoulder. "It's all right, Casey," she said. She looked at the others. "She's a little embarrassed about what happened yesterday."

"That's OK." Dylan stepped in front of the younger girl. Crouching down, she signed while she spoke. "We're happy to see you," she told her. "We have something for you."

She gestured for her friends to step forward with the accessories. As Honey handed her the brightly coloured scarf, Dylan explained that Casey could wear it as a headband.

"Here, I'll show you." She made a move to brush Casey's hair out of the way. Casey raised her hands as if to stop her, but hesitated, her eyes on the gorgeous scarf.

Dylan hesitated too, then gently carried on pushing Casey's hair aside. She caught her first glimpse of the cream plastic hearing aids in place behind the girl's ears but was careful not to react, instead simply tying the scarf in place so that it hid them from view.

"There," she said, rocking back on her heels and smiling with satisfaction. "That looks great. But wait, there's more!"

She helped Casey clip on the cute star-shaped earrings next, and then tuck the cap on top of it all. Casey's head was a little crowded, but she seemed delighted with her new accessories. The cap matched the colours in the scarf and the earrings sparkled at her lobes, matching the sparkle in her eyes.

Meanwhile Ms Carmichael had disappeared inside the barn. She re-emerged, leading the tacked-up Tiptoe and holding a riding helmet.

"Ready for your trail ride, Casey?" she asked.

Casey nodded eagerly and stepped towards Tiptoe. While Ms Carmichael and Jill were helping her replace the cap with the helmet and then mount, Dylan and her friends hurried in for their own ponies. Since Casey had never ridden on the trail before, Dylan was planning to lead Tiptoe for safety's sake.

"When you lead another horse from the saddle, that's called 'ponying'," she told Casey as she clipped a lead rope on to Tiptoe's halter, which had been left on beneath her bridle. "So that means I'm going to pony your pony!"

Casey giggled. Dylan was happy to hear her laugh again. She was also relieved that her hearing aids seemed to be working well even through the scarf, since it would have been really hard to tell the joke through signing!

Soon the five of them were heading along their favourite trail through the woods. Casey was staring around wide-eyed. She let out a little cry of surprise the first time a bird swooped past in front her, though Tiptoe barely flicked an ear at it.

"It's pretty out here, isn't it?" Honey asked the younger girl.

Dylan was afraid that Honey's soft voice and British accent might make it difficult for Casey to understand her even with the hearing aids. But Casey just smiled and nodded, then turned to stare at a pile of bright orange and yellow leaves.

When they reached their usual cantering spot on the trail, Morello pricked his ears and picked up his stride a bit. But Dylan half-halted him, keeping him at a steady walk.

Not today, boy. Sorry. We have more important things to do than break speed records.

She glanced back over her shoulder to make sure the other ponies were OK. They were all in the habit of blowing off steam during this stretch of trail, and while Minnie was unlikely to give Honey any trouble, Colorado and Tybalt were both much more apt to try to take matters into their own hooves. Luckily, however, everyone looked calm and content to continue the ride at the same slow pace.

"Should we turn back soon?" Malory asked. "We don't want to tire Casey out on her first trail ride."

"In a minute." Dylan looked ahead. "I just want her to see the river. And the Folly."

Soon they were at the river's bank. The water level had risen since their previous visit, so they came to a halt.

"You weren't thinking of crossing, were you?" Honey asked.

"Well…" Dylan shrugged.

"Forget it," Malory said flatly. "It's too high. Your aunt would kill us if she knew we took Casey across right now."

Dylan reluctantly agreed they were right. She definitely didn't want to scare Casey, especially since the ride was going so well.

"At least we can see part of the Folly from here," she said, pointing ahead. The trees had lost most of their screen of leaves by now, making it easy to see the stone tower rising from the clearing on the far side of the river.

Casey stared at it with interest. "It looks like a fairy

tale," she whispered, her words sounding muffled and run-together but clearer than before. "Like a magic castle where wishes come true."

"Yeah, it does, doesn't it?" Lani agreed. Then she started to tell Casey the story of how the Folly had come to be there. In the middle, she was interrupted by the loud, sharp cry of a hawk overhead.

Casey let out a gasp and tilted her head back. "What is it?"

"That was a hawk," Dylan told her. "A bird. There are all kinds of birds in these woods. Can you hear them singing?"

Casey tilted her head, listening. Then she reached up and pushed the helmet and scarf out of the way so she could adjust her hearing aids.

Dylan held her breath. The hawk's cry had faded away, but songbirds were twittering and chirping away all around. Would Casey be able to hear them?

Suddenly the little girl blinked, and her face was transfixed – first with attention, and then with delight. "Oh!" she cried. "I hear the birds! I hear them!"

Dylan wasn't someone who cried easily, but she felt tears gathering in her eyes as she realized that Casey was hearing birds sing for the first time in her life. She looked at her friends and could see by their expressions that they were moved as well. Even the ponies seemed to catch on to the significance of the moment. They stood perfectly still, only their tails moving to swish at flies. Tybalt didn't even react when a squirrel rustled in the trees, though normally such a thing might make him spook and spin. But now he seemed to relax and listen as a blackbird let out a gloriously melodic trill somewhere just off the trail. Casey heard it, too, and her smile widened even more.

Birdsong. It was just a little thing, something Dylan had always taken for granted – in fact, there had been times when she'd sleepily cursed the birds warbling outside her windows early in the morning. But now, watching Casey's expression of awe, hearing a bird sing suddenly seemed the most wonderful and important thing in the world.

Chapter Eight

The next afternoon, Dylan was still in a great mood thanks to what had happened on the trail ride. When she arrived at the yard for riding class, the first thing she thought about was how delighted and grateful Jill had been to see Casey's big smile and new-found confidence upon returning from the trail ride. The little girl had been more talkative than Dylan had ever known her, eagerly telling Jill with voice and hands all about hearing the birds.

"Thank you, Dylan," Jill had said, clasping Dylan's hand in both of hers. Then she'd extended her smile to the others as well. "Thank you, all of you!"

"Finally!" Lynsey exclaimed, her voice intruding into the pleasant memory as Dylan stepped into the barn. "It's about time we did some real jumping practice. We need it if we're going to have any hope of not embarrassing ourselves at the next show."

"What do you call those combination exercises we did last week?" Lani asked, rolling her eyes. "That wasn't exactly barrel racing."

Lynsey let out a snort. "Leave it to *you* to bring barrel racing into everything." With that, she disappeared into the tack room.

"Ignore her," Dylan told Lani. "She's just annoyed because she knows we're going to crush her at that ornament-selling challenge. Anyway, does this mean no dressage today?"

"Not for you, Malory and Lynsey," Honey replied, looking up from picking out Minnie's front hoof. "You guys are doing an extra jump school while the rest of us have dressage."

"Oh." Dylan felt a little thrill of nerves. This could only mean one thing – the next All-Schools League show was getting closer. With everything else that was going on lately, she'd nearly forgotten about it.

Soon she and the other two eighth-grade members of the Junior Jumping Team were warming up their ponies in the jumping ring along with the two seventh-grade members, who had given up a free period to be there. The other five members of Dylan's usual riding class had disappeared into the indoor arena with Mr Musgrave.

"Easy, Morello," Dylan murmured as she extended the pony's trot down the long side of the ring. Jumps were already set up in a course, and Morello kept trying to veer towards them, his attention more on the jumps than on his rider. It was obvious he had guessed what was coming.

"All right, everyone ready to get started?" Ms Carmichael called out after a few more minutes. "Gather around, please." When all five ponies were standing in front of her in a more-or-less straight line, she continued. "Now, I thought we could try a few easy courses today just to get back into the swing of things. You may remember we had a few difficult moments at the last show, and while it's nothing to get too worked up about, we can always strive to improve next time around."

Dylan grimaced and exchanged a glance with Malory. "A few difficult moments" was an understatement – the last show had been downright disastrous. However, she could tell her aunt was trying not to put too much pressure on them. She was always more concerned with growing and learning than she was with winning.

From the moment they started, it was obvious that all the riders wanted to prove that they could do better than they'd done at that show. Unfortunately, not all of them succeeded. While Lynsey and Bluegrass completed each course and exercise effortlessly, everyone else had trouble of one kind or another. Dylan fell into her regular trap of missing her line to fences coming out of tight corners. Tybalt got tense halfway around the first course and resisted all Malory's efforts to get him to relax after that. Joanna Boardman, who was riding her own pony, a bay Welsh cross named Calvin, kept reverting to her old habit of fiddling with his stride so much that they slowed to crawl before almost every fence. And Lucy Price, the team's reserve, fought with the talented but opinionated Skylark for most of the session.

"Ugh!" Lucy wailed once the girls were back in the barn untacking. "We totally sucked!"

"Speak for yourself," Lynsey commented smugly as she walked past with Blue's custom-fitted Devoucoux saddle balanced on her hip.

Lucy glared after her. "I *was*," she muttered.

"Never mind." As one of the senior members of the team, Dylan felt a responsibility to give pep talks to the younger girls when necessary. She glanced at Joanna, who looked just as glum as Lucy. "This is all part of the process. I mean, if we were perfect already, what would be the point of taking all those lessons?"

"That's right," Malory chimed in. "You guys did fine. As long as you learn from each mistake, you'll only get better. Anyway, like Ms Carmichael says, winning and being the best isn't the most important point of riding. It's probably not even in the top ten."

Dylan nodded. Normally she might have disagreed with that – especially coming from their team captain. True, the bond with a special pony was even better than the feeling of winning a blue ribbon. But why not aim to have both whenever possible? Lately, though, she'd started to wonder if she had been putting too much emphasis on competition and winning. What difference did it make who jumped a bunch of fences the fastest and cleanest? That couldn't possibly compare in importance to having great friends, a loving family, and good health...

"Dyl? You still with us?" Malory peered at her. "You're being awfully quiet."

Joanna laughed. "Yeah, anytime Dylan Walsh doesn't have anything to say for more than five seconds, something must be wrong."

Dylan grinned as Malory and Lucy laughed too. She was glad to see that the pep talk seemed to have worked – both seventh-graders looked more cheerful.

"Nope, I'm fine," she said, not quite ready to share her thoughts just yet, even with Malory. She slung her arm over Morello's neck. "Just enjoying hanging out with my favorite pone, that's all."

"I can't believe the seniors picked Lynsey's stupid hoity-toity crystal things." Dylan shot a look across the common room to the table where Lynsey and Patience were holding court over a pile of glass beads, feathers, and crystals, along with a couple of seventh-graders who had already been dubbed by Dylan as "Lynsey's minions" for the way they followed the snooty older girl around, hanging on her every word. The room was full to overflowing with girls working on prototypes for the holiday decorations they were planning to sell for the house fundraiser.

"Yeah, but they picked ours, too," Malory reminded her, bending over a piece of shiny red and silver paper she was cutting to the right size according to Honey's pattern. "These cracker things are a really neat idea, Honey."

"Thanks. I hope people like them." Honey swept her blonde hair out of her face and glanced over at a table where the rest of the Adams eighth-graders were working, including Razina. "Razina's bead garlands are going to be really great, too."

Lani nodded. "It's pretty cool that out of the eight designs they picked, three of them were suggested by eighth-graders. Go us!"

Dylan wrinkled her nose. "I prefer not to be lumped in the same category as Lynsey, thanks."

"There." Honey held up a sample cracker she'd just finished. It was a pretty tube-shaped package with bows on each end, covered with shiny blue wrapping paper. "That's about how it should look. Shall we show it to Miss Harvey?"

"She told us to call her Matilda," Malory reminded her. "And don't worry, unlike some adults, she means it. She's really cool."

Dylan had to agree with that. Matilda Harvey was the craft store owner Malory had mentioned at last week's meeting. She had already given the whole group a talk on the best ways to market their decorations and tips for increasing their efficiency in making them. Dylan had liked her immediately. She was about forty years old, with a perky brunette ponytail and a casual, friendly, down-to-earth demeanour.

"How's it going over here, girls?" Matilda asked as she came over. "Looks like you're working hard."

"We are," Malory said. "Honey just finished making a cracker, and the rest of us are getting close."

Dylan nodded. "We set up the table in stations, with piles of each thing we need, just like you suggested," she said, sweeping a hand to indicate the neat piles of wrapping paper, toilet paper tubes, ribbons and other materials.

"Terrific." Matilda smiled, her hazel eyes warm. "Now you guys are like a well-oiled machine, eh?"

At that moment Patience came running over with Lynsey sweeping along regally behind her. "We finished one," Patience announced, shoving an ornament in Matilda's face. "Isn't it awesome?"

Matilda seemed unperturbed by the interruption. "Very nice, girls," she said, taking the ornament and examining it from every angle.

Dylan wrinkled her nose, ready to adjust her opinion of Matilda if she really thought Lynsey and Patience's monstrosity was "very nice". The ornament was almost a foot long, with puffs of white and pink feathers drooping alongside some elaborate crystals and strings of pink and white beads. The whole thing was topped off with an enormous black-and-white striped bow.

"However," Matilda went on pleasantly, "you might want to consider scaling back the size a bit. It's a bit out of scale to the average ornament, which might limit your customer base."

Lynsey raised an eyebrow, as if scandalized that anyone would dare criticize her creation. "Actually," she said icily, "we've scaled it for a certain class of home. Not the tabletop tree market."

"Yeah," Patience put in with a sniff. "People with big houses and good taste will totally appreciate this kind of thing. Trust us, we know."

Rosie, who was making the rounds of all the work stations, arrived just in time to hear Lynsey's comment. "No, she's right, guys," the senior prefect said, taking the ornament for a closer look. "This is way too big. You'll have to charge thirty bucks a pop if you even want to make back the cost of the materials, let alone make a profit! I'd say cut it in half, at least."

Lynsey scowled. "Whatever," she muttered, not quite daring to argue with the confident, popular prefect. Then her gaze fell on Honey's sample cracker, along with the ones that the others had been trying to make. "I can't believe you guys chose *that* as one of the items. What's the point of them, anyway?"

"I'll show you." Honey took back the cracker she'd made from Matilda. Then she tugged hard on both ends. The cracker let out a sharp POP! that made everyone jump. When she tipped the now ripped packaging to one side, a boiled sweet, a tissue-paper crown and a slip of paper with a joke on it tumbled out of the interior tube.

Rosie laughed. "That's great!" she said. "I knew those would be fun as soon as you described them."

"Here, let me try mine." Dylan grabbed the cracker she'd just finished and gave it a yank. However, the paper just ripped without the popping noise. "Oh," she said, frowning. "Guess I didn't do it right."

"Never mind," Honey said. "I'll show you again." She picked up Dylan's failed cracker to examine it. "A-ha!" she declared. "The trick is to remember to put in the cracker snap." She pointed to the pile of little noisemaking devices on the table. They looked like thin strips of cardboard; they were treated so that when they were pulled apart at the pre-prepared join, they let out a snap.

Dylan groaned. "Figures I'd forget the most important part!"

"OK, so it makes a noise, big deal," Lynsey interrupted. "What does it have to do with Christmas?"

"Actually, these crackers are a big holiday tradition in England. Isn't that right?" Matilda shot a look at Honey, who nodded.

"We always had them," Honey said. "They're quite popular in other Commonwealth countries as well – Canada, Australia, New Zealand."

Lynsey rolled her eyes. "Whatever. Come on, Patience. Let's go see if we can, like, scale down our ornament without totally ruining it." Shooting Matilda and Rosie one last sour look, she stalked off with Patience following.

"It looks like you guys are on the right track here," Matilda said. "However, Lynsey does make one good point. Since Americans won't be as familiar with Christmas crackers, it might be a good idea to dress them up to look as Christmassy as possible. You know – choose red and green paper for the outside, perhaps tie some jingle bells on the ends or something…"

Lani was already nodding. "Sounds good," she agreed. "Right, guys?"

"Definitely!" the others chorused.

By the end of the evening, there was a large pile of finished crackers in the centre of the table. The other tables had made a lot of progress on their designs, too. The girls stored all the completed decorations in boxes along the wall beneath the windows and left the tables tidy and well stocked with materials, ready for the next evening's session.

"Good job, everyone," Matilda called out with a wave. "Keep it up. And I'll be looking forward to seeing your display at the Christmas Fair next week!"

She waved and left to cheers and calls of thanks from all around. "She's really nice," Honey said. "I'm glad you thought to bring her out, Malory."

"Mm-hmm." Malory was staring after Matilda, looking thoughtful. "And you know, I never really noticed before, but she's really pretty. I wonder if she's got a boyfriend."

"Looking for a date, are you, Mal?" Lani raised an eyebrow. "Caleb will be jealous if he hears."

Malory grinned. "Very funny. No, I'm thinking about my dad."

Dylan gasped. "That's perfect! Matilda looks about his age, right?" She was always happy to get involved in any sort of matchmaking – even when it involved old people – though she couldn't help being surprised that Malory had brought it up. "Um, not to be nosy," she added. "But does this mean you're, like, ready for your dad to start dating?"

"Yeah. Not *too* nosy, Walsh." Lani smirked.

Luckily Malory didn't seem to mind the question. "I don't know," she admitted as the four of them wandered toward the door. "It's hard, I guess. I mean, sometimes it seems like yesterday that my mom died, and it's totally weird to imagine him with anyone else. On the other hand, he's got the rest of his life to live. It doesn't seem fair that he should be on his own." She shrugged. "Anyway, if he has to get together with anyone, Matilda seems like a good choice, right?"

"Absolutely," Honey agreed.

Dylan laughed. "Ah, I see I'm finally rubbing off on you! Who needs romance when you can live through everyone else's gossip!"

Chapter Nine

Dylan tapped at the computer keys in front of her, feeling restless. She shot a glance down the line of monitors in the Study Centre. Malory and Honey were gathered at one computer, laughing softly and taking turns typing. Lani was at another, crouched over the keyboard. Dylan didn't even have to ask what they were doing. They'd been trading IMs with the boys for the past twenty minutes.

Once again, she found herself feeling left out, even though she knew her friends didn't mean to make her feel that way. *Somehow, this boyfriend thing was more fun when it was still in the matchmaking stages,* she thought. *Now that they're all paired off and happy, it's actually pretty boring, at least for me.*

She immediately felt guilty for thinking like that. After all, she was thrilled that her best friends were so happy. It would be nice if she had something better to do during their Tuesday afternoon double study hall than watch them giggle and flirt, that was all. The girls had all finished their homework within the first half hour, and then they'd decided to try to contact the boys. Dylan had tried to IM her cousin Nat, who was a student at Saint Kit's, but he wasn't online.

Logging off, Dylan stood up and stretched. "Be back in a minute," she said to the others, who barely looked up. "I'm just going to look for a book to read."

She wandered off to the stacks and chose a row, walking along the cool, musty aisle and running her fingers along the spines of the books. Deciding to pick something to read at random, she closed her eyes and pointed to a book.

"Ugh," she muttered when she pulled it out. It was a well-worn old leather-bound copy of a history of the US Postal Service.

Deciding that a different row might suit her better, she hurried around the corner and looked at the first set of titles. *A-ha, much better*, she thought when she saw that she was in the animal section.

She was making her way towards the horse books when she paused, her eye caught by the illustration of a brightly coloured bird on one of the spines. All around it were other books about birds. Dylan scanned the titles and selected one about the birds of Virginia. Flipping through it, she saw that it had clear colour photos and descriptions of the sounds made by each local bird. Her mind had already jumped back to that special trail ride on Sunday.

"Casey would love this," she murmured, her finger tracing the illustration of a bright-red cardinal.

On impulse, she tucked the book under her arm and

hurried back to her friends. "I'm going to cut out a little early," she told Lani. "Cover for me?"

Lani glanced up. "Sure. Where are you going?"

"I'll tell you later." Now that she'd set her mind on what she wanted to do next, Dylan was eager to go. "Thanks, Hernandez."

"No prob." Lani's gaze had already wandered back to the screen, where another line of type had just appeared. If Honey and Malory had even noticed Dylan's presence, they gave no indication of it.

A few minutes later Dylan was riding down the long, sweeping Chestnut Hill entrance lane on a bicycle borrowed from the small collection kept by Adams House for the use of the students. The bird identification book was in the lightweight backpack over her shoulders. The drive sloped downward for much of the way between Adams and the main gates, and she coasted along enjoying the brisk autumn wind against her face.

The two-mile trip to Cheney Falls took quite a bit longer on the bike than it did on the bus, but even so Dylan was soon gliding to a stop at the curb in front of Cheney Manor. She'd remembered the address printed on the side of the minibus, and had no trouble locating it in the small town. She looked up at the place, which turned out to be located in a rambling old redbrick Victorian house. The building looked a bit shabby, with a few loose tiles, paint peeling on the shutters, and one window repaired with duct tape. But the small, square, autumn-leaf-strewn lawn was neatly mowed and the front door was painted a cheerful shade of sky blue.

"Dylan!" Jill exclaimed in surprise when she answered the door. "What are you doing here?"

"I decided to drop in and see if I could visit Casey," Dylan replied, a bit breathless after the long ride. "I borrowed this really great bird book from our school library, and I wanted to show it to her, since we had so much fun listening to birds together on our trail ride the other day."

"Oh, how thoughtful! She'll love that!" Jill beamed and stepped back, opening the door wider. "Come on in and I'll show you to her room."

Dylan looked around curiously as she followed Jill down the narrow, high-ceilinged hallway and up a broad staircase to the second floor. Although the exterior of Cheney Manor could be described as drab, no one would have dared use that word in connection with the inside. Vivid floor-to-ceiling murals covered most of the walls, and the wooden floors were covered with bright rag rugs. The scents of cookies, tuna fish, and Lysol mingled together in a surprisingly pleasant way. Overall, the whole place had a friendly, homey feel to it.

It's sad that there are kids without homes of their own, Dylan thought. *But if they can't live at home with their families, at least they get to live here.*

While they walked, Jill gave a running tour of the place, pointing out a playroom for the younger kids and a library stocked with shelves of well-thumbed books and several ancient but still serviceable computers that had been donated by the local public high school.

"We appreciate whatever donations of goods and services we get," she explained. "If we can't use them directly, we sell them to raise funds for the things we do need." She winked. "And of course, cash is always our favourite gift!"

"Mine too," Dylan joked with a grin, feeling more glad than ever that Adams House had decided to support Cheney Manor for their charity project.

At the end of the second-floor hallway they reached another staircase leading to the third floor. The hall up there was even narrower, but with the same bright murals, rugs, and well-worn but functional furniture. Jill stopped in front of a door with a picture of a horse taped on the outside.

"Here we are," she said.

Dylan pointed to the picture. "I should have guessed!"

Casey, who was wearing jeans, a T-shirt, and her new head scarf, looked just as surprised to see Dylan as Jill had been. At first she seemed cautious, even a bit suspicious. But when Dylan explained why she was there and pulled out the book to show her, Casey's face lit up.

"Come in," she pronounced carefully.

"I'll leave you to it," Jill said. "Let me know if you two need anything."

"Will do." Dylan gave the woman a wave, then followed Casey into her room. "Wow, nice place you have here!" she said when she took a look around.

Casey smiled. "Thanks."

The room was small, with space for little more than a bed, a desk, a small bookcase, and a dresser. But every inch of the walls was covered with animal pictures from magazines or posters. There were tigers, koalas, dolphins, dogs and too many other species to count. Most of all, there were horses and ponies – dozens of them, of all shapes, sizes and breeds.

"It must've taken you ages to hang up all these," Dylan commented, peering at a picture of a Grand Prix jumper. Suddenly realizing she'd been facing away from Casey when she said it, she turned, ready to repeat herself.

But Casey was nodding, and Dylan guessed she must be wearing her hearing aids beneath the scarf. Honey's plan had worked!

After admiring the walls for another few minutes, Dylan sat down cross-legged on the floor with the girl beside her. They paged through the book looking at the photos of birds and talking about what they saw. Conversation was much easier due to the hearing aids, and Casey was full of questions, especially about the sounds the birds made. Dylan tried to imitate some of the birdsongs she knew, but finally she threw up her hands.

"I'm terrible at this!" she exclaimed with a laugh. "Why don't we just go outside and see what we can hear out there? There are plenty of birds that live in town; I'm sure we can identify a few."

Casey nodded eagerly. "There's a park on the next

block," she said, her words so fast and excited that Dylan had to concentrate to make them out. "Maybe we can go there!"

"Great idea." Dylan picked up the book, and the two of them headed back downstairs.

Jill was in the kitchen stirring something in a pot on the stove while one of the other employees peeled potatoes at the table nearby. When they heard about the proposed outing, both women nodded.

"Do you have a mobile phone in case you run into any trouble?" Jill asked Dylan.

"Of course." Dylan never went anywhere without her BlackBerry, though she always made certain to turn it off during class so it wouldn't get confiscated. "Don't worry, we'll be careful."

"All right, then have fun." Jill touched Casey on the arm. "Listen to Dylan and do as she says, OK? And be back in time before dark."

It was early dusk already, but the street and park were both well lit. Dylan and Casey had a great time listening for birds and trying to spot and identify the ones they heard. Dylan had a pen and some paper in her backpack, and she gave them to Casey to record their sightings. Within a few minutes they had half a dozen birds identified and written down. Dylan didn't even protest when Casey insisted on noting a "possible encounter" with a red-throated loon – though Dylan was pretty sure the eerie hooting sound had come from a passing car's radio!

Soon it was nearly dark. "Ugh," Dylan said. "That's

the worst thing about this time of year – the days just keep getting shorter."

"Yeah," Casey agreed. "It stinks even more if you're deaf. It's hard to see what people are signing in the dark!"

Dylan laughed, appreciating the joke that only Casey could have come up with. "Come on, let's head back," she said, tucking the book in her pack. "Speaking of signing, maybe you can teach me some more ASL, OK?"

Back at Cheney Manor, they checked in with Jill and headed upstairs to Casey's room again. They spent a while practising sign language. Dylan was getting better at it all the time, and Casey taught her some of the nuances and also helped her practise her finger spelling.

Dylan found herself warming to the younger girl more and more. Casey was smart and observant, which she'd already known. What she hadn't known was that she had a sly sense of humour! Now that she seemed to trust Dylan, she teased her whenever she made an error in her signing, and was quick with a joke at her own expense, too.

The two of them were laughing over Dylan's latest mistake – she had mixed up two of the new signs Casey had taught her, and had accidentally said that she liked to eat new clothes when she'd meant to say she liked to shop for new clothes – when there was a knock at the door. Jill stuck her head in.

"Casey, dinner," she said. "Oh! Dylan, you're still

here! I assumed you must have headed back by now – it's getting late."

Dylan glanced at her watch. "Oh my gosh!" she exclaimed, jumping to her feet so fast that she knocked her backpack off Casey's bed. "It's almost seven o'clock! I'm going to be in huge trouble!"

"Oh dear." Jill looked concerned. "Well, you certainly can't ride your bike back in the dark – let me give you a lift. Should you call someone to let them know you're coming?"

Dylan had already pulled out her BlackBerry. She realized she'd never turned on the ringer again after leaving her last class, and a glance was all it took to see that she had received nineteen new voicemail messages in the past couple of hours.

"No, that's OK," she said grimly, stuffing the BlackBerry back into her backpack and slinging the pack over her shoulder. "I'll just wait and hear them yell at me in person."

She said goodbye to Casey and hurried downstairs with Jill. After shoving the bike in the back of Jill's hatchback, they headed out of town.

"Sorry I lost track of time," Dylan said, staring out at the darkened country road as the lights of Cheney Falls faded behind them. "I didn't want to put you out."

"It's no trouble," Jill assured her. "I'm just so glad you've taken such an interest in Casey. You're really bringing her out of her shell! All she can talk about these past few days is birds and ponies."

Dylan smiled. "She sounds like me and my friends at

school. Well, except that we don't talk about birds that much."

Jill chuckled and hit the turn signal, slowing for the turn into Chestnut Hill's drive. "The ponies are wonderful therapy, aren't they? Not just for Casey – all the kids are benefiting from their lessons here. I only hope Casey will be able to continue with that once she leaves us."

Dylan blinked, wondering what she meant by that. Before she could ask, she saw flashlights bobbing just ahead. "Uh oh," she muttered. "I have a bad feeling about this…"

Sure enough, when Jill slowed and opened her window, the flashlights turned out to belong to a search party out looking for Dylan. When the head security guard saw that she was safe and sound, he immediately called in to his boss with the news.

"Sorry about that," Dylan told him, glad that the darkness hid her bright-red face. "I didn't mean to worry everyone."

When they pulled up in front of Adams, Dylan thanked Jill for the lift and grabbed the bike out of the back. She was wheeling it towards the storage shed when her friends came running.

"Where have you been?" Honey cried.

Lani frowned. "Yeah, Walsh. When you said you were taking off early from study hall, I didn't think you meant you were running away from school, too!"

"Plus you missed our team practice this afternoon." Malory put in.

Dylan's heart sank. As if she wasn't already in enough trouble, she'd totally forgotten that Ms Carmichael had called for another Junior Jumping Team practice that day after classes.

"Sorry," she said. "I guess it just slipped my mind. But listen, I saw Casey today, and—"

She didn't get any farther. The Adams housemother, Mrs Herson, had just hurried out the main doors.

"Dylan Walsh!" she thundered. "I hope you have a *very* good explanation for this!"

Chapter Ten

Unfortunately, Dylan's explanation didn't seem to satisfy Mrs Herson very well. Or Ms Carmichael, either, who arrived at Adams House a few minutes later. After both of them had yelled at her for a while, Dylan was sent upstairs to her room.

"I'll bring up your dinner on a tray in a few minutes," Mrs Herson added sternly. "You're grounded until further notice – no leaving your room for anything but your classes, meals and visits to the bathroom until I say so."

"Yes, ma'am," Dylan said meekly.

"And we'll continue this discussion tomorrow, Dylan," Ms Carmichael added with a frown. "Compared to everything else, missing team practice is a minor misdemeanour. But I'd still like to have a talk with you about it. Come down to the yard and see me during your first class break."

"OK," Dylan whispered, feeling tears gathering in her eyes. "Thank you both for not killing me."

Mrs Herson pursed her lips. "That hasn't been ruled out yet."

Dylan wasn't sure whether that was supposed to be a joke or not, so she didn't dare laugh. Instead, she turned and scurried for the stairs.

Up in her room, she shut the door behind her and flopped on to her bed without bothering to turn on the lights. Fortunately Lynsey was nowhere to be seen; after everything else, Dylan wasn't sure she could tolerate her roommate's smirks and snarky comments without throwing her out the window. And she was in trouble enough without adding attempted murder to her list of offences.

Why oh why don't I ever stop and think before I do things? she wondered bleakly, staring up at the ceiling. *It's like I get so focused on one thing that I forget about everything else, never mind the consequences.*

A moment later there was a tentative knock on the door. "Dyl?" Lani said, sticking her head in. "We just wanted to make sure you're all right."

"I'm fine." Dylan let out a loud sigh and rolled over on her stomach to look at them. "You'd better not let anybody catch you talking to me, though – I don't want you guys to get in trouble."

Honey and Malory were peering in, too. Malory grimaced. "Yeah, we heard some of the yelling."

"The whole state of Virginia probably heard it," Lani said.

Honey gave her a poke. "Hush! Dylan feels bad enough already."

"Come on," Malory said. "Dylan's right, we aren't supposed to be here. Besides, we'd better get down to the common room before they start the DVD without us."

Dylan waved as they left, wistfully imagining the fun of DVD movie night in the common room. Still, for once she didn't even think about sneaking out of her room to join in the fun. She knew she'd messed up big time. Not going off campus without telling someone was the number one boarding school rule, and she hadn't only broken it – she'd smashed it to smithereens.

I didn't even tell my friends where I was going, she thought miserably, rolling on to her back again. *I went by myself – another no-no – and I stayed out after dark. Strike three. No wonder Mrs Herson looked ready to blow her top!*

With a sigh, she got up and changed into her pyjamas. Then she sat down at her desk, trying to take her mind off her predicament by focusing on studying for her upcoming French test. But the words just swam on the page in front of her, not making any sense at all.

Just as she was about to give up, there was a brisk knock on the door and Mrs Herson came in carrying a tray. "Here you go," she said, setting it on the desk beside Dylan's books.

"Thanks." Dylan forced a smile.

Mrs Herson sat down in Lynsey's desk chair. "I forgot to mention it before, but I called your parents earlier when we thought you'd gone missing."

"What?" Dylan was horrified. It had never occurred to her that her parents would be brought into this, and she felt more terrible than ever for causing them that kind of worry. "Um, do they know—"

"Yes, I called them after I'd spoken to you to let them know you were back safe and sound. But you'll want to call them yourself and reassure them."

"Um, OK," Dylan said half-heartedly. "I'll call them tomorrow."

"No, I think tonight would be better. You need to face up to what you've done and how much danger you put yourself in."

Dylan nodded mutely, not trusting her voice at the moment. Tears sprang to her eyes again as she realized the true seriousness of that afternoon's impulsive decision. She tried to fight them back, not wanting the housemother to see her cry, but a few squeezed out and trickled down her cheeks.

"I'm sorry," she choked out at last, her voice shaking. "I really didn't mean to worry everyone. I – I guess I just didn't think, and I knew Casey would love that book, and…"

Mrs Herson sighed. "Oh, Dylan," she said, her expression softening slightly. "I know you're terribly impulsive and generous – it's what makes you such a unique addition to this dorm." She shook her head. "But I can't help recalling that it's gotten you in trouble before."

Dylan bit her lip, guessing that the housemother might be thinking about the time the previous year when Dylan had sneaked out to ride Morello in the middle of the night. She'd been in big trouble for that stunt, too.

"I'm sorry," she said again.

"You're not a child any more, Dylan," Mrs Herson said. "You really need to work on learning what is appropriate behaviour and how your decisions impact the people around you, as well as yourself." She stood up and headed for the door. "Now call your parents, and then eat."

Dylan did as she was told. Predictably enough, her parents were furious with her. "You're getting too old for this, Dylan," her father said.

"*Much* too old," put in Dylan's mother, who was on another extension. "I think we'd better make sure you understand how serious this is, young lady. That's why you won't be coming with us to the Christmas show at Radio City Music Hall this year. Instead, you can stay at home and think about growing up a little."

Dylan bit her lip. She loved her family's annual trip into New York City to see the holiday lights. She always made jokes about how cheesy the famous Christmas Spectacular was, especially the high-kicking Rockettes. But in truth, she loved every minute of it. It would be terrible to miss it this year, but she knew better than to protest or try to change her parents' minds. After all, this was all her own fault.

"OK," she whispered, clutching the phone to her ear. "I'm sorry."

"But I still don't understand. Why didn't you tell us where you were going, Dylan?" Malory stirred her cereal and stared sombrely at Dylan.

Dylan shrugged, playing with her toast. She and her friends were sitting at their usual table eating their normal breakfasts. But that was the only thing that felt normal. The others were acting kind of awkward, obviously not quite sure how to treat her after everything that had happened.

"For the millionth time, I don't know," she said. "I just didn't stop to think about it."

Honey shook her head. "But you must have realized," she said. "I mean, you had to go all the way back to Adams, get out the bike…"

"Ride all the way into town," Lani picked up. "Find Cheney Manor. Stay there all afternoon until it got dark."

"Yeah." Dylan sighed. "I was there, OK? I remember what I did."

"But you didn't answer my question," Malory insisted. "Why in the world didn't you just say something to us about where you were going?"

Because you were all too busy IMing with your stupid boyfriends! Dylan thought with a flash of annoyance.

But she didn't say it out loud. For one thing, she didn't want to alienate the only people who weren't currently furious with her. Besides, she knew she wasn't being fair. If her friends' behaviour had bothered her or made her feel left out, she should have either talked to them about it or just gotten over it. After all, that sort of thing had never bothered her before. How were they supposed to guess if that had changed?

"You're right, I totally should have said something,"

she said. "I just got carried away and didn't stop to think about what I was doing."

Malory sighed and dipped her spoon back into her cereal bowl. "Well, I hope it doesn't happen again. None of us can afford to miss any more practices, especially between now and the show on Saturday."

"I know, I know."

"I'm serious, Dylan," Malory said. "We really need to make up some points considering how terribly we did last time. Otherwise we'll end up last in the league."

Dylan could hardly believe how seriously Malory was taking her duties as team captain all of a sudden. Since when did she care so much about winning? Dylan had thought that Malory, if anyone, might understand that some things were way more important.

But she didn't bother to say anything about that. "Yeah, I know," she said instead, hoping Mrs. Herson and Ms Carmichael would still let her ride on Saturday. "Don't worry, Morello and I will be ready for the show. We won't let you down."

After that, the others started talking about the fundraiser. But Dylan hardly listened. She finished her breakfast as quickly as possible, then told her friends she'd forgotten a book in her room as an excuse to leave early.

"Hey, boy," Dylan murmured, reaching up to scratch Morello in his favourite itchy spot under his mane. It was later that morning, and she was on her way to her meeting with Ms Carmichael. It felt strange to be in the barn wearing her school uniform of royal-blue kilt and sweater, grey blazer, and black penny loafers instead of the more usual jeans and paddock boots.

Morello snuffled at her, leaving a trail of white hairs across the front of her sweater. Then, finding no traces of carrots or peppermints, he ducked his head back into the stall to take a bite of his hay.

"Oh, my gosh." Dylan frantically brushed at the hairs. The school took tidiness and personal responsibility very seriously – Lani had once been formally reprimanded for walking around with the school crest half falling off her blazer due to loose threads. Dylan could only imagine what Mrs Herson and school principal Dr Starling would say if they could see the current condition of her own uniform. That would probably be all they needed to decide to ship her off to Alcatraz!

"Ah, Dylan. There you are." Ms Carmichael had just hurried into the barn carrying a couple of empty buckets. "Time for our meeting already? This morning has flown by! First I had to bring in horses for the farrier, and then Kingfisher managed to give himself a cut on the fetlock somehow and Soda ripped his turnout blanket half to shreds… But never mind all that." She set down the buckets and gestured for Dylan to follow. "Let's go to my office."

Dylan followed, still picking at the hairs. Somehow, no matter how many she picked off, three more seemed to appear to take its place! By the time they reached the office, Dylan felt as if she'd made no progress at all.

"Here," Ms. Carmichael said, reaching into her desk drawer and pulling something out. "Try this."

Dylan looked up and saw that her aunt was holding up a lint brush. "Oh!" she said. "Um, thanks."

"You're welcome." Ms Carmichael smiled wryly. "Having one of those around is pretty much a requirement of the job. Especially when big donors or important alumni want to see the barn, and Dr Starling expects me to be neat as a pin despite wrestling thousand-pound, sweaty, hairy, often obstinate beasts for a living. And for once I'm *not* referring to you students. For one thing, none of you are anywhere near a thousand pounds."

Dylan smiled back. She rolled the lint brush over her sweater and the lapels of her blazer. Before long, she was clean and tidy once again. Whew!

When she handed back the lint brush, Ms Carmichael tucked it away and then went serious again. "Now, Dylan," she said, sitting down in the chair behind her desk. "What are we going to do about you?"

Dylan could normally come up with half a dozen clever answers to that sort of question. Today, however, she had the feeling it might be safer to hold her tongue.

Ms Carmichael tapped her fingers on the desktop. "I'm sure Mrs Herson has covered the obvious dangers of waltzing off alone like you did," she said. "As your aunt, I'll just add that if you ever do anything like that again, I'll kill you myself. However, as your Director of Riding, I'll move on and address the issue of missing practice yesterday."

"I'm really sorry about that," Dylan said. "You know I hardly ever forget anything to do with riding. For some reason, it just totally slipped my mind that we were having that extra practice. And you don't even have to tell me – I know I let myself down."

"That's right. But the thing is, you didn't only let yourself down. You let down your fellow team members as well. Not to mention Morello, who's going to be expected to perform at that show on Saturday without as much practice as the other ponies."

Dylan bit back a sigh at yet another reminder of how irresponsible she'd been. Did they all have to keep pounding that into her head over and over again? She *got* it!

However, she couldn't help a flutter of guilt at the thought of failing Morello. He did deserve everything she could do for him, considering how he always poured his heart into performing his best at shows.

And I suppose Aunt Ali is right about letting the others down, too, she thought with a hidden sigh. *I don't want to fail them, either. Well, except maybe Lynsey…*

"Don't worry, Ms Carmichael," she said, filled with new resolve. "I'll do everything I can to make up for this. Maybe I can put in some extra schooling time between classes or something?"

"No, that's all right, Dylan." Ms. Carmichael shot her a half-smile. "Somehow, I expect extra riding time might not seem like much of a punishment to your housemother. You're lucky I convinced her you needed to ride in the show for the sake of the rest of the team.

So just show up at tomorrow's practice ready to do your best and we'll see if we can let bygones be bygones, all right?"

"You've got it," Dylan promised. "I'll be there – one hundred and ten per cent. You can count on it."

Chapter Eleven

"I think I'm finally getting the hang of this." Lani held up the Christmas cracker she'd just finished.

Honey took it and examined it. "Looks great, Lani. Did you remember to put in the snap?"

"Of course she did," Malory joked as Lani nodded. "Making noise is Lani's favourite thing!"

"You know it." Lani grinned and let out a loud whoop, making the girls at several nearby tables look up in surprise.

"This is a civilized common room, not the rodeo," Lynsey called over to her irritably.

"Yeah," Patience added. "Keep it down, cowgirl."

"Never mind them." Dylan made a face as the pair turned away. "They're just annoyed because they know we're going to beat the pants off them raising money for Cheney Manor."

It was Wednesday evening, and the residents of Adams House were hard at work once again making decorations. Since it was for charity, Mrs Herson had agreed that Dylan could take part, even though she was still grounded from all her other extra-curriculars except the riding team. Honey, Lani and Malory were much better at making the crackers than Dylan was, so she was helping Razina's group by stringing some of their beaded garlands.

Dylan had thought she'd kept her voice down while making the last comment, but apparently she wasn't quiet enough for it to escape Lynsey's sharp ears. "Excuse me, Dylan?" Lynsey said. "I must be going deaf. Because I would swear I heard you claim you were going to raise more money than me. Which is obviously crazy."

The reference to deafness irritated Dylan, and she shot back without thinking, "Dream on, Lynsey. You know it's true."

"Right." Lynsey rolled her eyes. "I'm *so* sure people are going to be fighting over your little homespun toilet paper trinkets when they could have some of our one-of-a-kind designer ornaments instead, made by hand from the finest materials on the East Coast."

"Did you hear?" Patience added. "Lynsey's mother sent us some more stuff – a bunch more beads and crystals, and also these cool pink silk tassels. Aren't they gorgeous?" She held up a tassel, which looked as if it belonged on the end of a lamp cord.

"Very nice," Honey said politely. "In any case, it's good that we'll have a variety of ornaments for people to choose from. We'll sell more that way."

"Right. Something for everyone," Malory added.

Lynsey shrugged. "I suppose. Maybe you'll sell a few

of those snapping things to little kids. That might bring in a few cents here and there."

Dylan gritted her teeth, seething at her roommate's obnoxious attitude. On the one hand, Lynsey's stupid pink and black ornaments were completely ridiculous. On the other hand, she *did* sort of have a point. If she managed to con anyone into actually buying her snooty junk, the high price tag she was likely to charge for them would add up quickly.

Luckily, Patience and the other minions are so incompetent that they probably won't end up finishing many of those things, she thought. *All we have to do is make sure we have tons of merchandise to sell by showtime.*

That thought inspired her to put on a burst of speed. If she finished this batch of beads, she could go back to helping with the crackers. Even if she wasn't that great at wrapping and finishing them, she could at least cut the paper to size so the others could work faster…

"Ack!" she cried as she tried to jam another bead on to the almost-finished garland … and ended up losing hold of the whole thing instead. She grabbed for it, but it was too late. It fell to the floor, sending beads bouncing everywhere.

"Oh, no!" Malory said. "Here, we'll help you gather them up."

"No, it's OK." Dylan dove for the floor and crawled under the table, scrabbling for the rolling beads. "Just keep working. I've got it covered."

"Haste makes waste, Dylan," Lynsey said with a smirk.

Dylan didn't bother to answer. If she did, she knew she'd probably say something that would land her in front of Mrs Herson again. And Lynsey Harrison definitely wasn't worth it.

"Brr!" Joanna Boardman said as she trotted Calvin across the diagonal. The whole team was in the jumping ring warming up for the final team practice before the show. "It's getting chilly out here."

"Yeah. And we're not the only ones who've noticed," Malory commented grimly as Tybalt spooked at a scattering of wind-blown leaves and then threw in a small buck for good measure.

Dylan kept her leg on Morello, making sure he was paying attention to her and not allowing him the option of taking Tybalt's antics as an excuse to act silly himself. All the ponies were on their toes and extra alert. Even Bluegrass had let out a few snorts and swivelled his ears around upon entering the ring, though he had settled down as soon as Lynsey put him to work. It was already getting dark, and the artificial floodlights left odd shadows here and there that bothered a few of the ponies. Skylark in particular seemed very suspicious of a certain dark bar left by the light post in one corner and kept trying to jump the shadow every time Lucy rode her around that side.

Ms Carmichael strode to the centre of the arena and clapped her hands. "All right, everyone," she called, having to raise her voice more than usual to be heard over the wind. "We're going to continue where we left off on Tuesday. That last grid we did then should have helped remind the ponies to rock back on their haunches on takeoff. So let's test that with the course I've set up here. It looks simple, but it has a few tricky spots, so don't take anything for granted. Malory? Why don't you give it a try first? The rest of you, watch and learn."

She didn't make any reference to Dylan's absence on Tuesday, and for that Dylan was grateful. It was going to be hard enough playing catch-up, especially since it sounded as if she'd missed some interesting and useful exercises and not just the usual practice courses.

"Here we go, boy," she murmured to Morello as she nudged him into motion. "Let's see if we can figure out what we missed by watching."

She rode over to the far end with the others while Malory began the course. Tybalt was still wild-eyed and distracted and tried to run out on the first jump. But Malory kept him moving forward, swerving him back into line and urging him on. The jump was a bit awkward and Tybalt's hind legs hit the top rail with a *thunk*, which spooked him all over again for a few seconds. But after that he seemed to remember what he was doing – and that he should trust Malory – and they finished the course without incident.

Lynsey and Joanna got around fairly easily as well. The session Dylan had missed the other day seemed as if it had paid off for her teammates; they were all riding confidently despite the weather, looking well prepared for Saturday's show.

When her turn came, Dylan gathered up contact and sent Morello forward into a warm-up circle, aiming for a bouncy, collected, but impulsive canter. The pony fought her throughout the circle, first scooting forward above the bit and then slowing down and losing most of his impulsion. In a show, Dylan knew she would have to aim for the first fence and hope for the best. But since this was just schooling, she circled a second time. And this time she managed to connect with Morello, finally maintaining the canter she wanted, though it took most of her strength to hold him together.

"Nicely done," Ms Carmichael called as the pair finally turned toward the first obstacle.

Dylan didn't dare lose concentration by acknowledging the compliment, even with a smile. She pushed her pony forward, not wanting to miss her distance and risk taking down a rail. As a result, they ended up too close to the first fence; luckily Morello was more than athletic enough to cope, and they sprang over the rail with inches to spare. To Dylan's relief, they ended up going clean over the rest of the course as well.

Whew, she thought as she pulled up, feeling sweat pooling beneath her helmet. *At least we didn't embarrass ourselves this time*.

She managed to keep up throughout the rest of the session as well – barely. By the time Ms Carmichael called for them to cool out their ponies and put them away, Dylan's arms were aching from trying to hold Morello back, her legs from creating impulsion, and her entire body from half-halting like crazy to keep him together. It was amazing that missing one key practice had left her feeling as rubbery and weak as they all did whenever they came back after a school break or at the start of a new semester.

Her pony, too, was showing the signs of working extra hard to make up the lost ground. His head hung low, his sides heaved, and his neatly clipped brown and white coat was slick with sweat.

"Is it OK if I sponge him off in the wash stall?" Dylan asked as she slid down and walked Morello over to Ms Carmichael a few minutes later.

"Yes, good idea," her aunt replied, casting a critical eye over the pony. His breathing had returned to normal but he was still sweaty. "When you're finished, throw one of the coolers from the tack room over him and leave him in his stall. I'll check him later and put his blanket back on when he's dry."

Dylan nodded and gave Morello a pat. "Come on, boy," she said. "Bath time." Even though she was exhausted herself, she never even considered sitting down to rest until her pony was comfortable.

Soon she was sponging and scraping the pony's coat in the wash stall at the end of the main barn. It was warm inside the barn thanks to the body heat thrown off by its four-legged residents, and Morello seemed to be enjoying his bath. Steam rose from his coat, and he nosed curiously at the bucket of water at Dylan's feet. The rest of the team's ponies hadn't been as hot as Morello, so their riders had already put them away and left, with Malory promising to save Dylan a spot in the cafeteria if she was late for dinner. Dylan was hungry and badly in need of a shower, but she was taking her time, enjoying the private time with her favourite pony.

"Hold still, wriggle worm," she ordered as he tried to turn sideways in the cross-ties. "Don't worry, I'll get to your other side in a minute."

Morello stood still, occasionally flicking his tail at the trickles of water running under his belly. Dylan hummed as she worked, enjoying the feeling of the barn, vacant except for her and the horses. It made her feel more peaceful than she had for the last few days.

Just as she was reaching for the cooler she'd hung over a bar on the wall nearby, Morello suddenly snorted and pricked his ears at something in front of him. "What is it now?" Dylan asked with a laugh.

She followed the pony's gaze, expecting to see a leaf blowing down the aisle or perhaps one of the barn cats stalking past. Instead, she saw a girl's face peering around the corner of the wash stall at her.

"Oh!" she cried, jumping in alarm before realizing it was Casey, which surprised her even more. "Oh wow, you startled me!"

"Sorry," Casey said and signed, stepping into full view. She was dressed in jeans, sneakers, and a worn-looking nylon jacket, plus the colourful scarf and Lani's pink hat. Her face was pinched with worry.

Dylan tossed the sweat scraper she'd been using into the bucket and stepped towards the girl. "Hey, what are you doing here?" she asked. "Cheney Manor isn't scheduled for a late-evening lesson I didn't hear about or something, are they?"

Casey shook her head. Her lower lip trembled as she lifted her hands to sign something, but her signs came so fast and furious that Dylan had no hope of keeping up.

"Whoa, slow down," she said. "I didn't catch that."

Casey made the sign for "terrible". After that she just clenched both hands into fists and turned away.

Dylan bit her lip. Whatever was going on, it was clear that Casey was very upset. You didn't need to know ASL to see that.

"Hang on a sec," she said, grabbing the cooler and quickly slinging it over the damp pony. "Let me put Morello in his stall, and then we can sit down and talk."

Minutes later Casey was sitting on one of the tack trunks in the heated tack room, a cup of cocoa Dylan had just made in the feed room's battered microwave held in both hands. "OK," Dylan said, settling on another trunk with her own cup. "Now let's try this again. Tell me what's going on – slowly."

Casey nodded. Taking a deep breath, she started explaining in a combination of signs and spoken words. She explained that she'd heard Jill talking to one of the other adults about how someone else would be moving into Casey's bedroom soon.

"They must," she blurted out. "They must…" She stopped, making the sign for sending away.

"You think they're sending you away?" Dylan frowned. "But why would they do that? That's crazy."

Casey shrugged. "Some of the kids go to special

schools," she said. "But I don't want to go. I want to stay. I like my room, and riding Tiptoe, and writing down birds..."

Her eyes filled with tears and she resorted once again to signing, her hands moving so quickly that Dylan was left behind. All she could make out were the signs for "horse", "bird" and "no".

Meanwhile Dylan had just flashed back to her car ride home to Chestnut Hill with Jill on Tuesday night. With everything else that had happened immediately afterward, she'd all but forgotten. But Jill's words came back to her now: *I only hope Casey will be able to continue with that once she leaves us.*

So it's true, Dylan thought with a sharp ache of sadness. *They must be shipping Casey off to some kind of school for the deaf or something.*

She felt angry for a second, then swallowed a sigh as she realized there was no point in that. It had been great getting to know Casey; Dylan was going to miss her like crazy. Still, as the older and supposedly wiser person in the room, she knew what she had to do. Whatever had led the Cheney Manor people to this decision, surely they had Casey's best interests at heart. Maybe Dylan could help her understand that and accept it.

"I think you're right," she told Casey honestly. "Jill said something about it to me the other day, though I didn't understand what she meant at the time. Still, don't look so sad – this is actually great news!"

Casey stared at Dylan as if she'd sprouted a spare toe

in the middle of her forehead. "No," she said. "I don't want to go."

"But it'll be great." Dylan set down her cup and leaned forward, forcing a cheerful smile. "Maybe you'll go to a really cool school like Chestnut Hill, where you can make tons of new friends. Kids who are, you know..."

"Kids who are like me?" Casey snapped. "Deaf?"

Dylan felt her face turn red as she realized that was exactly what she'd been thinking. "Um..." she said, suspecting she'd just made things worse instead of better.

At that moment the tack room door swung open. Ms Carmichael walked in and stopped short when she saw them, looking surprised.

"Oh," she said. "No wonder I smelled hot chocolate. I thought the ponies must have finally figured out how to use the microwave. That Colorado always has had a sweet tooth."

Dylan was sure that such a remark normally would have made Casey giggle. But the younger girl couldn't manage anything more than a wan smile. She stared down at her cup, looking as if she wished she could crawl into one of the tack trunks and disappear.

"How did you get here, Casey?" Ms Carmichael asked, taking a step closer and looking concerned. "Did Jill bring you by?"

Casey shook her head without looking up. "I walked," she whispered, her words more garbled than they'd been recently but still intelligible. "I know the way. I paid attention in the minibus."

Dylan blanched at the thought of the little girl hiking the long two miles along the isolated country highway between Cheney Falls and Chestnut Hill. *Maybe riding that bike into town didn't set such a good example*, she thought guiltily.

Her aunt shot her a look, making Dylan suspect that she was thinking the same thing. "Come along," Ms Carmichael said, holding out one hand to Casey. "I'll drive you back. I'm sure they're worried about you. Dylan, can you give them a call to let them know we're on our way?"

"Sure," Dylan said, reaching into her jacket pocket for her BlackBerry. "Bye, Casey! See you at your next lesson."

But Casey didn't respond or even look back as she trudged away at Ms Carmichael's side.

Chapter Twelve

Dylan woke up on Saturday morning to the sound of rain rattling against the windows. "Oh, great," she muttered, wiping the sleep from her eyes and sitting up. "Just what we need."

It was the day of the All-Schools competition, and Dylan had the blisters and aching muscles to prove it. The entire barn staff, plus the members of the jumping teams and as many additional volunteers as they could scrounge up, had spent hours the previous afternoon preparing to host the show. Ms Carmichael always kept the stables and rings tidy, but for a show she insisted on an extra level of spit and polish. The main and warm-up rings had been dragged and raked, the jumps had been dusted off and their paint touched up as necessary, fresh pine branches had been tucked into the fence fillers, the entire stable yard and both barns cleaned from top to bottom, and every equine on the place groomed within an inch of its life, including the retired old school pony Coal, who mostly just hung out in his field and wouldn't even be seen by most of the competitors. In the end all the hard work had been worth it; Chestnut Hill was ready to put its best foot forward in playing host to the other seven schools in the league.

However, now it seemed the weather had started things off on a sour note. Dylan didn't really mind riding in the rain – Chestnut Hill's jumping ring had excellent footing that wouldn't be affected by anything short of a monsoon – but Morello hated getting wet and tended to shake his head non-stop at every raindrop.

Still, there wasn't much Dylan could do about the weather. She climbed out of bed and started getting dressed, glad that at least one thing was going her way so far – Lynsey was already up and out of the room.

"There you are." Ms Carmichael looked distracted as Dylan and her friends burst into the barn, soaked to the skin by the driving rain despite running all the way from Adams. "We're moving the show course to the indoor ring. It's a bit smaller than ideal, but it will have to do under the circumstances."

"See? Told ya." Lani elbowed Dylan in the side. "So Prince Morello won't have to get his dainty self wet."

Dylan just nodded, too breathless to respond. All through breakfast, Lani and Honey had done their best to boost the spirits of the two members of the Team. Even so, neither Dylan nor Malory had eaten much.

"Do you need us to help move the jumps?" Malory asked Ms Carmichael.

"Thanks, but Kelly and Sarah already took care of it." The riding director was looking past the girls towards

Senior Jumping Team member Jillian Watt, who was struggling to hold on to a clearly hyped-up Soda further down the aisle. "Unfortunately, we'll still have to make do with warming up out in the rain. Just do your best."

"I'm soooo nervous!" Joanna Boardman wailed, rushing down the aisle just then carrying Calvin's bridle. "Plus my brand-new Vogel boots are soaked through – I stepped into this puddle on the way down that I swear was, like, waist deep!"

"Look on the bright side, Jo," Anita Demarco, captain of the Senior Team, called over from the wash stall. Her own horse, the flashy chestnut gelding Prince of Thieves, was standing calmly in the cross-ties while Anita braided his neatly pulled mane. "Since your boots are brand new, getting wet while they're on should end up making them fit you like a glove. Just be sure to leave them on until they're totally dry."

"Easier said than done in this weather," Lani muttered, casting an anxious glance out the open end of the barn, where sheets of rain were still coming down.

Dylan followed her gaze. Even through the rain and gloom, she could make out the shapes of the vans and trailers from the other schools, which they'd passed on the way in. All around the trailers, students from those schools were milling around, walking their horses or huddling beneath the trees at the edge of the parking lot.

"Check it out," Dylan said. "Looks like the team from Two Towers has rainsheets and hoods for their horses in their school colours. The riders have all got matching jackets and helmet covers, too. Pretty sharp."

Malory barely spared a glance outside. "This is no time for talking about fashion, Dyl," she said, sounding tense. "Let's get the ponies tacked up so we can be ready to warm up if there's a break in the rain."

Unfortunately, the break in the rain never came. Half an hour later Dylan found herself squinting to see past the rain dripping off the rim of her helmet as she rode Morello around the rail of one of the outdoor rings. "Wish I had one of those fancy rainsheets right about now," she muttered, holding both reins in one hand long enough to yank up the collar of her plain old non-school-colours raincoat, which she'd pulled on over her show clothes. The hood wasn't quite large enough to fit over her helmet, which meant that every few seconds a rivulet of rainwater found its way down the back of her neck.

Oh well, she thought, shivering as another dribble hit the small of her back. *At least my helmet isn't velvet, so it won't get ruined even in this deluge.*

She cast a sympathetic glance toward Joanna, whose velvet Charles Owens hat was encased in a plastic shopping bag as she rode Calvin around the soaked outdoor ring with an unhappy look on both their faces. Just then Morello tossed his head so violently that he almost bonked Dylan in the nose, which quickly brought her back to reality.

"OK, calm down," she told the pony, kicking him forward. "Let's just warm up and be done with it, and hope I won't regret not putting a standing martingale on you."

By the time she finished a quick warm-up and reached over from Morello's saddle to let herself out of the ring, Dylan had been unable to avoid noticing that the riders from the other teams looked much more energetic and well prepared than she felt. The riders from Two Towers Academy were still wearing their matching gear, which also turned out to include waterproof quarter sheets. Sienna Macleod, a very successful A-circuit junior who was on the Allbright's team, was warming up her fancy show pony over much bigger fences than anything she would encounter in the ring that day. Malory's boyfriend Caleb, one of the top riders on the Saint Kit's team, looked calm and competent as he popped his horse George over several jumps and then did a few leg yields and shoulder-ins down the long side of the ring.

Bet none of them *missed any practices this week*, Dylan thought wryly.

"Wait for me," Malory called as Dylan was about to let the gate swing shut behind her. "We're done, too."

Dylan held the gate while Malory steered Tybalt through. She wasn't sure which of them looked more like a drowned rat – the girl or the pony. Tybalt's tail was plastered to his legs, which seemed to irritate him, as he kicked out several times. His braids looked limp and bedraggled. So did Malory. Dylan was sure she looked just as pathetic herself.

"This is miserable," she said as the two girls hurried their ponies towards the shelter of the barn's narrow overhang, only dismounting once they were mostly out of the rain. "Why couldn't we have nice weather like we did last weekend?" She sighed wistfully, remembering that wonderful trail ride through the woods to the Folly.

"Focus, Dyl," Malory said, running up the stirrups on Tybalt's saddle. "We've got a show to do."

Honey came running out of the barn, wrapped in her rain jacket with the hood pulled up over her head. "There you are!" she said, joining Dylan and Malory under the overhang. "Ms Carmichael wants you to meet her in the indoor arena." She reached for Morello's reins. "I'll take him back in the barn for you and scrape off as much water as I can."

"Thanks." Dylan handed over the reins just as Lani appeared behind Honey and offered to do the same for Tybalt.

Soon Dylan and Malory had joined the rest of the Junior Team in the indoor ring. The rain pounded on the roof, making a lot of noise, but the ring looked tidy and serene. Nobody would have guessed it had been called into use at the last minute. The jumps looked colourful and imposing, and the sand underfoot was raked to perfection. Several riders dressed in the navy team jackets of Lindenwood Country Day School were already walking the course.

"Good, everybody's here," Ms Carmichael said as her five Junior Team riders gathered at the end of the ring just outside the gate. "I wanted to talk to you all before it's time to get started. I realize it's kind of chaotic, what with the weather and everything. But don't let that rattle you, all right? You're all well prepared for this, and I know you can handle today's course."

"I would certainly hope so," Lynsey said. "I'm just hoping some of the less experienced and spookier ponies don't let us down due to the rain and everything." She shot a glance in Malory's direction.

Malory ignored the jab, keeping her gaze on Ms Carmichael. But Dylan clenched her fists at her sides in irritation. Lynsey had had it in for Tybalt since he'd arrived at Chestnut Hill. Just because he wasn't a blue-blooded, perfectly made show pony, she seemed to think he was worthless.

Then again, she's never exactly been crazy about Morello, either, Dylan thought. *Or Colorado. Or most of the other school horses…*

Realizing that her aunt was speaking, she tuned back in. "…so I just want to remind you that we're a team," Ms Carmichael was saying. "Every performance counts, and you owe it to one another to try your best. And to yourselves, and your ponies, of course. Just remember that the weather will disadvantage the other teams equally, so no excuses. All right? Then let's do this!"

The two seventh-graders let out a ragged, rather nervous-sounding cheer. Dylan pumped her fist and threw in a "whoo-hoo".

"Can we walk the course now?" Malory asked.

Ms Carmichael nodded. "Good luck, everyone. Just ride your best and you'll be fine."

The Lindenwood riders were just leaving, so the Chestnut Hill team had the course all to themselves for the moment. Dylan walked out into the ring with the others, vainly trying to keep the sand from sticking to her wet boots.

"Whoa," Lucy said when the little group reached the first jump, a vertical. "This looks really big."

"Yeah," Dylan agreed. "But never mind that – check out the crooked line to jump two."

Malory nodded. "That's going to be a tricky one to take. We all might want to walk it off a couple of different ways so we're prepared no matter what kind of jump we have over the first one."

From there, the course didn't get any easier. In fact, Dylan was pretty sure it was the biggest, twistiest one they'd showed over yet. Even Lynsey looked rather pale and kept her snotty remarks to a minimum as she carefully measured out the striding between each jump.

When the class started, their worries were borne out. Dylan watched the first two riders go – one from Wycliffe College, and the second from Saint Kit's – and both of them had problems. The Wycliffe girl messed up the striding on the crooked line and ended up barely clearing the second fence at an awkward angle, which resulted in a runout at fence three. The second rider did OK on the first three fences, but his small, round pony had trouble with the width of some of the oxers and brought down two rails.

Dylan had drawn number fourteen in the line-up, so as the third rider was coming in, she left to grab Morello out of the barn for their final practice. Her stomach was jumping with nerves as she rode out into the rain once more. Malory was already in the outdoor ring trying to soothe a frazzled Tybalt, who spooked and snorted every time a Two Towers rider passed too close with one of their flapping quarter sheets.

Meanwhile Morello kept humping his back and skittering to one side or the other, shaking his head. Dylan knew he wasn't trying to be naughty – he was just distracted by the rain on his face and the wind blowing under his tail.

"Come on, boy," she told him, urging him into a trot and doing her best to ignore the almost constant shaking of his head. "We'll get this over with as soon as possible and get back inside where it's dry."

She had just taken the pony over a warm-up fence a few minutes later when she noticed someone running through the rain towards the ring from the direction of the parking lot. To her surprise, she saw that it was Jill from Cheney Manor.

Riding Morello over to the rail, Dylan called out to her. Jill hurried over, looking anxious.

"Dylan!" she panted, rain dripping from her waterproof hat. "I'm glad I found you. You haven't seen Casey, have you?"

"What? No, not today," Dylan said. "Didn't anyone tell you? All lessons and other outside riding is cancelled today because of the show."

"Oh, I know," Jill said. "It's not that. Casey ran away!"

"What?" Dylan gasped.

Jill nodded, gulping to catch her breath as she leaned on the wet wooden rail. "When I went to wake her for breakfast this morning, she wasn't there. Her bed hadn't been slept in, and there was a note on it that said she didn't want to go away to 'the deaf kid school' – she wanted to stay where she was."

"Oh my gosh!" Dylan exclaimed.

"I don't know where she got the idea we were sending her away to school," Jill went on. "There are no plans to send her to any special deaf schools."

Dylan bit her lip, suddenly feeling very guilty. "Um, actually she and I talked about that a couple of nights ago when she came here," she admitted, clutching her reins tightly. "She overheard something, and then I mentioned what you said to me in the car…" She quickly told the whole story to Jill, who looked devastated. "I'm sorry," Dylan added at the end. "I should have said something to you at the time. And I definitely shouldn't have made her think she was right about being sent away without checking with you first."

Jill sighed. "Thanks for telling me now, at least," she said. "I'd better go find your aunt and let her know what's happening. If Casey is trying to make her way back here to Chestnut Hill in this terrible weather…"

She didn't bother to finish the thought. Dylan watched her hurry towards the indoor arena, then gathered her reins and headed for the gate to follow her.

Soon she was listening to Jill explain the problem to Ms Carmichael. "Please," Dylan put in, sliding down from the saddle. "Let me help search for Casey. I've gotten to know her pretty well lately; I might be able to figure out where she might have gone."

"Thank you, Dylan," Jill said. "But the police are handling it." She glanced at Ms Carmichael. "Casey's mother is dead, but she has some contact with her father, who lives in Chicago. The police are checking all the local bus terminals and train stations to see if she's trying to get to him. I just thought I'd check here as well, since she ran here the other day."

Dylan couldn't help shuddering at the thought of Casey all alone at some dingy bus terminal trying to make her way halfway across the country, especially when she couldn't hear properly. "I'm sure she wouldn't do that," she said. "But I could check around here some more just in case—"

"That's enough, Dylan." Ms Carmichael shot her niece an annoyed look. "It sounds as if you've done quite enough already."

Dylan's heart sank. "But..."

"Come on, Dyl," Lani said, grabbing her by the arm and pulling her away while Honey took Morello's reins.

Dylan hadn't even realized her friends were there listening until that moment. She stared at them, feeling frantic. "But we have to find Casey!"

"You can't. Besides, you've got a team counting on you." Lani gestured to the ring, where Malory had just ridden in to start her course.

Honey nodded. "You're up right after this, remember?"

Dylan stared out at Malory, who rode Tybalt confidently over the first jump and met the second one perfectly. "But I want to help search," Dylan said.

"There are lots of people out looking for Casey," Lani said firmly. "Adults. Experts. They'll find her. In the meantime, you need to get your focus back on this competition, stat."

Dylan frowned. She wanted to argue that a riding competition didn't seem that important all of a sudden. But at that moment the announcer came on, congratulating Malory on her clear round and calling Dylan in for her turn.

Feeling trapped, Dylan mounted Morello, barely noticing as Lani checked the girth and Honey gave her boots a swipe with the rag she was holding. Before she quite knew what was happening, she found herself cantering towards the first fence.

Focus, Walsh, she told herself, snapping back to the here and now. *Your friends are right. You have no more idea of where Casey might be than anyone else, so there's no point in messing up the whole team over it.*

After that, she somehow managed to block out her worries about Casey and ride. It wasn't the smoothest or most elegant course she and Morello had ever laid down – they bungled the crooked line and had to put in an extra stride to fence three, and only Morello's honesty and athleticism saved them from a rail at fence five – but somehow they made it over the first three-quarters of the course with no faults. Dylan knew she wasn't in danger of winning any equitation prizes, but that didn't matter. All that mattered was going clean, and now there were only a few more fences to go...

"Easy, boy," she murmured as Morello landed from

a wide oxer, half-halting to set him up for the next obstacle, a gleaming white gate with wings painted to look like grey stone towers.

As they cleared it, it was as if a little light bulb suddenly went on over Dylan's head. She let out a gasp, almost forgetting what she was doing as she realized exactly where Casey might have gone…

She barely heard the announcer congratulating her on her clear round as she rode out of the ring and straight out the arena doors. "Dylan, wait!" Lani called, hurrying to catch up with her with Honey at her heels. "That was awesome!"

Honey nodded, beaming. "We knew you could do it."

"Never mind that." Dylan shot a glance around to make sure her aunt and Jill were nowhere in sight. "Listen, I think I just figured out where Casey is! I've got to go!"

Ignoring her friends' protests, she kept going, kicking Morello forward as soon as they reached the grass on the far side of the pathway. Morello was sweating after his tough jumping round, but he gallantly broke into a canter and then a gallop. The rain was still coming down in sheets, making it hard to see as they headed across the yard into the woods. Dylan winced as she heard the boom of thunder in the distance.

"Hang on, Casey," she muttered. "I'm coming…"

It was a harrowing ride through the trees. All the trails were waterlogged, making the footing tricky, and branches were whipping and cracking in the gusty wind.

147

The thunder got closer and more frequent, and every few minutes the sky was lit up by flashes of jagged lightning. Dylan just crouched down over Morello's neck and urged him on, letting the brave and sensible pony choose his own path.

Finally they reached the river. Morello skidded to a halt on the bank and Dylan blinked the rain out of her eyes, staring forward in shock. The river was swollen and angry-looking, white-capped eddies flinging themselves up well over the usual waterline. Still, Dylan knew they had to get across.

"Come on, boy," she urged Morello. "You can do it. It'll only come up to your tummy."

Morello danced in place as she squeezed firmly with both calves, his head stretched forward as he stared at the rushing water. It was obvious that he thought it was a bad idea to go near the river in its current state. But finally his trust in Dylan won out, and he cautiously stepped forward, first picking his way into the shallows and then plunging forward, splashing quickly to the other side.

"Good boy!" Dylan shouted, giving him a pat before kicking him on again. "Almost there…"

She pulled him to a stop in Folly's Glade and flung herself out of the saddle. Then she hurried towards the tower entrance, dragging Morello behind her.

The interior of the tower was cold, damp … and empty. Dylan squinted in the dim light, refusing to believe her eyes. She'd been so sure…

As soon as she'd seen those tower-shaped wings on

either side of fence eight, she had been certain that Casey would be here. It sounded as if Casey barely knew her father. Why would she try to get to him, when all she really wanted was to stay where she was – near Chestnut Hill? And what better place to hide than the spot where she thought wishes came true? The Folly that looked like it belonged in a fairy tale.

But now Dylan slumped, trying to accept that she'd been wrong. Casey wasn't here.

Suddenly Morello pricked his ears and tilted his head, staring upwards in the direction of the blocked-off staircase. Dylan glanced at him.

"Did you hear something, boy?" she whispered, straining her own ears while wishing they were as sensitive as a horse's. With his keenly developed sense of hearing, Morello would be able to make out the tiny footsteps of a mouse or squirrel. Then again, he would also be able to hear something much bigger…

Dylan dropped her pony's reins, leaving him ground-tied where he was. Then she sprinted for the steps, ignoring the sign and ducking under the chain that was supposed to keep people out.

"Casey?" she called as she hurried up the rough spiral steps, almost slipping several times in her wet leather boots but not letting that slow her down. "Casey, are you up there?"

The weak grey daylight coming in through the tower's narrow upper windows was enough to reveal Casey's small form huddled against the far wall. Dylan rushed to her.

"Casey!" she cried, not sure whether to laugh or cry in her relief. "You're here!"

Casey looked up, her small face grubby and her expression wretched. She was wearing her head scarf, earrings and baseball cap. Her backpack was lying open beside her, and Dylan could see that the only thing in it was the bird book she'd lent her.

"I won't let them send me away," she said with a sob, her words so muffled that Dylan could hardly understand them. "I don't want to go away to school!"

"Oh, Casey, I'm sorry." Dylan bent down and gathered her into her arms, hugging her tightly. "I got it all wrong – we both did. They're not sending you away after all. It's safe to come home, OK?"

It took a bit more convincing than that, but eventually Dylan coaxed the younger girl down the steps. Casey seemed a bit surprised to see Morello standing there.

"He'll help me take you home," Dylan told her. "I know he's no Tiptoe, but I think you two will get along great."

She took off her helmet and put it on Casey's head. It was a little too big, but Dylan did her best to adjust the chin strap and figured it would have to do. Then she led Morello back outside.

It was still raining, though the thunder had faded into the occasional grumble in the distance. Morello walked along obediently across the clearing and down the first part of the trail with Casey riding and Dylan leading.

But when they reached the riverbank, he planted his

feet and started to back up. "Come on, buddy," Dylan said, tugging on his reins. "We just did this, remember? You can do it again."

But Morello was putting his hoof down this time. No matter what Dylan did, he wouldn't go within two yards of the rushing water. Casey clung to his wet braids, her eyes getting wider and wider as the pony swung his hindquarters from side to side, flung his head, and continued trying to back up.

"Come *on*!" Dylan shouted, tears of frustration mixing with the rain on her cheeks. What was she supposed to do now? For once her quick, clever, scheming mind failed her. She realized she didn't even have her BlackBerry on her to call for help, since she was still in her show clothes.

"Dylan!" a shout came from across the river.

Dylan gasped and looked up, hardly daring to believe her eyes. There on the far bank, mounted on their ponies, were Lani, Honey and Malory!

Chapter Thirteen

"He won't cross!" Dylan shouted to her friends.

"Hang on!" Lani kicked Colorado forward. He was the bravest of the three ponies on the opposite bank, and it wasn't long before he was fighting the current towards them. The other two ponies seemed alarmed to be left behind; Tybalt tossed his head and jumped around a little, while Minnie just lowered her head and stared anxiously after Colorado. But Dylan knew her friends could handle them. She focused on Morello and Casey.

"Lani will lead us back across," she told Casey. "Morello will want to be with his stablemates, so he should definitely go now. Just hang on tight and don't look down, OK?"

Casey nodded and wrapped her hands even more tightly around Morello's braids, which were coming loose. For once Dylan was grateful for her sloppy braiding job. That would give Casey more to hang on to.

The trick worked. As soon as Lani turned Colorado back across the river, Morello plunged in after him, not wanting to be left behind. Dylan hung on to his bridle and went with him, praying she didn't trip on a rock or step in a hole underwater. The water was up to her waist, cold and fast-flowing, threatening to drag her away every time she lifted one foot up to take a step. But Morello braced his neck to keep her in place, and by the time they reached the other side he was practically dragging her along.

Seconds later all four ponies were safe and sound beneath the shelter of some thick evergreens on the near shore.

"How did you find us?" Dylan asked her friends, collapsing against Morello's side. Her boots were full of the river, her jodhpurs clung to her like ice-cold skin, and her valuable wool jacket was black with water marks, but right now all she could think was how grateful she was to her friends and Morello for getting her across.

"You're not the only smart one around here, you know," Lani told her with a grin.

Honey nodded. "After you ran off like that, we put our heads together to try to figure out where you'd gone."

"We realized there was only one hiding place on campus that Casey knew about," Malory finished. She glanced up at the younger girl, who was still clutching Morello's mane. "Now we'd better get her back before they call out the National Guard or something."

Dylan nodded. "Mind if we ride double?" she asked Casey, hoping that Morello wouldn't protest.

"I've got a better idea," Honey said. "Why doesn't Casey ride with me? Minnie isn't as tired as Morello."

Dylan nodded, realizing that Minnie was also quieter than Morello and less likely to act up in protest of being ridden double. "OK," she said, helping Casey dismount from Morello's back and then hoisting her up to sit behind Honey's saddle.

"Wrap your arms around my waist and hold on tight," Honey told the girl. "Don't worry, Minnie's trot is as smooth as silk."

Dylan then swung aboard Morello, trying not to think about what her aunt would say if she caught her riding without a helmet. *Still, might as well keep Casey's brain safe instead*, she thought. *I won't need mine once they all finish killing me for running off again.*

"Let's take it easy," Malory suggested as she turned Tybalt to head back through the woods. "The footing's pretty bad out here. Besides, Tyb and Morello have a jump-off round to do once we get back, so we should save their energy."

Dylan grimaced. She'd nearly forgotten about the show. After what had just happened, it was hard to wrap her mind around the fact that it was still going on.

They managed to keep the ponies at a ground-covering trot most of the way back. When they reached the woods closest to the barn, they encountered a search party consisting of four or five riders, including Caleb from Saint Kit's. The searchers were relieved to see the girls, and explained that a lot of people were out hunting for them even as the show continued.

"Great," Dylan said weakly. "So much for sneaking back in without anyone noticing we were gone…"

Caleb pulled a mobile phone out of his raincoat pocket. "I'll call and tell them we're on the way."

Jill was waiting for them at the edge of the yard. "Casey!" the woman cried, tears streaming down her face. "Oh, darling, we were so worried about you!"

Casey stretched out her arms, already crying as well. Jill pulled her gently down from behind Honey, and the two of them hugged each other tightly.

Dylan smiled as she watched. No matter how much trouble she got in for riding off like that, it had been worth it.

"Dylan! Malory!" Ms Carmichael had just appeared in the doorway of the indoor. "Get in here! Your rounds are next!"

Neither of the girls had any time to prepare for their next round, which was timed. All Dylan could was give Morello a pat as they headed for the ring gate, hoping she could remember the shortened jump-off course after only a quick glance at the diagram.

"Don't worry, buddy," she whispered to him. "I know you must be worn out. We'll just take it easy and aim for a slow and steady clear, OK?"

As she gathered up her reins, the pony snorted and tossed his head, seeming to come alive. He even jigged a bit as she walked him into the ring, making Dylan smile.

Has there ever been such a super-duper, extra-special, lion-hearted pony as this one? she thought, her heart swelling with pride. *I'm lucky just to know him, let alone get to ride him!*

Sure enough, Morello rose to the challenge and jumped a clear round over the course. It wasn't as fast as it might have been if he hadn't just galloped and trotted a few miles down a muddy wooded trail and forded a raging river, but it wasn't bad.

"I'm so proud of you, boy!" Dylan cried, bending forward to give the pony a big hug around the neck before sliding down and running up her stirrups. Honey hurried forward with Morello's cooler slung over her arm, and Dylan quickly pulled off the saddle and threw the cooler over his back.

Lani was standing nearby watching the ring. "Here goes Mal," she said.

Dylan turned to watch with the others. Tybalt walked into the ring and cantered calmly through the timers.

"Wow," Lani said as the pair cleared the first fence. "I think that's the first time I ever saw Malory having to kick him on."

Honey nodded. "Look at him, though," she said. "He's responding – they're really going fast now! But he's super calm and focused."

It was true. Tybalt zipped around the course without any of his usual tenseness or head flinging, barely looking at the fences but just jumping whatever Malory pointed him at. She ended up taking the short way between two of the obstacles, and executed an impressive turn to another, shaving even more seconds off their time. As they passed the time again, the viewers let out a cheer.

Tybalt had just laid down the fastest jump-off round so far!

"Wow," Lani said, sounding impressed. "Maybe Mal needs to take Tyb for a crazy rain-soaked trail ride before every round!"

Dylan shuddered. "Maybe not," she said. "I'm going to take Morello back to the barn – let me know what I miss, OK?"

By the time she finished grooming and pampering her pony and returned, the final Chestnut Hill rider, Joanna Boardman, was on course. Dylan's friends told her that Lynsey and Bluegrass had beaten Malory's time by half a second, which Lynsey would no doubt be endlessly smug about. But right now, that didn't matter as much as the fourth member of their team performing well. Dylan held her breath along with the others as Joanna finished the course. She, too, had gone clear!

There was only one more rider after that, and before long Ms Carmichael took the announcer's microphone to announce the results. "Finishing in first place, we have the junior team from Alice Allbright's," she said. "Congratulations, girls! And second by just a few points is your host school, Chestnut Hill…"

Dylan didn't hear anything after that; she was too busy screaming and dancing around along with the rest of the team and all their supporters. In the middle of their celebration she noticed Casey and Jill standing with the other spectators nearby. She smiled and waved, glad that Casey had been allowed to stay and watch the rest of the competition. Casey waved back, though Jill didn't appear to notice Dylan; she was busy talking into a mobile phone.

Probably calling the police and everybody else who was helping with the search, Dylan thought, her smile fading. *I just hope Casey doesn't get in too much trouble for this. After all, it was partly my fault that she ran away in the first place. I showed her the Folly, and I encouraged her to think she was being sent away to school.*

She was still thinking about that half an hour later when she found herself in the yard office with her aunt and Mrs Herson. They had called her in for a meeting as soon as she'd finished taking care of her pony.

"I'm sorry," she blurted out before they could speak. "I know I've been saying that a lot to you guys lately, but I really, really mean it. I did a dumb and dangerous thing today, and as usual it was because I didn't stop to think. I was just so worried about Casey…"

"We know, Dylan." Mrs Herson leaned against the edge of Ms Carmichael's desk, arms crossed. "And Casey is lucky to have a friend like you who cares so much about her. You're also lucky to have such good friends who were willing to risk punishment themselves to come out to help you."

"I know," Dylan said humbly, realizing just how true that was. "I hope you won't hold this against them. It's really all my fault."

Mrs Herson's mouth twisted up in a half-smile. "That's very noble of you, Dylan. You did a very brave thing today, if perhaps not the smartest thing in the world. But I may be able to overlook it and not involve

Dr Starling this time if you promise never to do anything so foolhardy again."

"I promise!" Dylan said quickly. "Um, at least I promise to try. Really, really hard."

Mrs Herson chuckled, but Ms Carmichael still looked serious. "I agree with Mrs Herson, more or less," she said. "I'd just like to point out that you also put Morello at great risk, Dylan."

Dylan bit her lip. "I know," she said, thinking yet again what a special, brave, loyal pony Morello was. She was lucky her aunt had brought him to Chestnut Hill with her and even luckier that she'd been allowed to ride him. She tilted her chin up, trying to be brave. "I'll understand if you don't want to let me ride him any more."

"Don't be silly, Dylan," her aunt replied with the ghost of a smile. "Yes, you acted impulsively today, but at least you did it out of loyalty – to a friend, not just a team or a competition."

This time she smiled for real and winked. Dylan felt warm inside as she realized the truth – her aunt hadn't come right out and said it, but it was pretty obvious she was proud of Dylan for putting her concern for Casey ahead of her competitiveness in the show.

"Still, I suppose we should come up with some sort of punishment," Mrs Herson spoke up, glancing at Ms Carmichael. "We wouldn't want the other girls to think we've gone soft and they can get away with anything."

"Mmm," Ms Carmichael agreed. "But what sort of punishment?"

Dylan held her breath, visions of lost riding privileges and other such horrors dancing through her mind. Both Mrs Herson and her aunt were well known to be kind but strict…

"I know," the housemother said. "How about if Dylan has to do some volunteer work on the weekends? Say, every Sunday afternoon for the next couple of months?"

Ms Carmichael nodded. "That sounds like a perfect idea," she agreed. "And I know the perfect place that could use the help – Cheney Manor."

Dylan's eyes widened. "Really?" she said. "Oh wow, that would be awesome!"

"Careful," Mrs Herson warned, her eyes twinkling. "Don't look too happy about it, or we might have to change our minds and make you scrub pots in the dining hall instead."

"Right," Ms Carmichael said. "We wouldn't want anyone to think we've gone soft."

Back at the dorm, Dylan found her friends waiting for her in the foyer. "So?" Lani demanded as soon as Dylan entered. "Are you grounded for life, or what?"

"Nope." Dylan shrugged off her rain jacket. "But don't worry, I'll never pull a stunt like that again!"

Malory looked sceptical. "At least this week, right?"

Dylan laughed, then flung her arms out, sweeping all three of them into a group hug. "Thanks for coming to save me, you guys," she said. "I know you took a big risk doing that."

"We never even thought about that," Honey told her.

Lani nodded vigorously. "You're our best friend," she said. "We *had* to come!"

"Right," Malory agreed. "We're always here for you, Dylan. You know that."

Dylan nodded. She *did* know that, and she was grateful. It was nice to have such loyal friends. They were a team, and that was a good feeling.

Just then Lynsey came sweeping down the stairs. She stopped short when she spotted them.

"Well, look who it is – Miss Pony Express," she said disdainfully. "See? I always knew that spotted thing you ride would be better off as a stunt pony, Dylan." She rolled her eyes. "It's a sheer fluke we managed to win enough points to come in second after you showed such a complete lack of loyalty to the team."

Dylan was ready to retort, but Malory beat her to it, stepping forward to get in Lynsey's face. "That's enough, Lynsey," Malory snapped. "As team captain, I can say you're way out of line. You wouldn't know loyalty if it jumped up and licked you in the face."

Lynsey blinked, stunned into silence by normally mild-mannered Malory's reaction. Finally she shook her head and spun on her heel.

"Whatever", was all she could come up with as she stomped back toward the stairs.

Once she was gone, Dylan grinned. "Way to go, Mal," she said, raising her hand for a high five. "Riding through the rainy stormy woods and fording a river is one thing. But *you* just achieved the impossible – you actually got Lynsey Harrison to shut up and go away!"

Chapter Fourteen

"Ready to go?" Honey stuck her head into Dylan's room the next morning.

"Coming." Dylan shoved her feet into her favourite Merrell slip-ons and hurried into the hallway to join her friends. All four of them were heading down to the common room to pack up the decorations they'd made. The Cheney Falls Mall's Christmas Fair started that day and they wanted to be there as soon as it opened.

Halfway down the hall from the common room, they heard the hubbub. Several people were talking loudly, sounding upset.

"What's going on?" Lani wondered, putting on an extra burst of speed.

Dylan did likewise and was right on her heels when Lani burst into the room. A bunch of girls were gathered around the boxes they'd stacked under the windows.

"What's going on?" Dylan called to Rosie, who had both hands to her head and looked horrified.

The prefect spun to face them. "It's the decorations," she cried. "We must have forgotten to shut the windows last time we were in here, and with all that rain yesterday—"

"Everything is ruined!" Ansty van Sweetering wailed, picking up a bedraggled-looking ornament.

"Not quite everything," Razina corrected, digging into one of the boxes. "We might be able to save a few of the beaded garlands. Maybe some of Lynsey's ornaments, too, if we take the feathers off."

Lynsey scowled. "They won't look right without the feathers."

"Well, they won't look right with sopping wet ruined feathers, either," Alexandra Cooper pointed out.

Dylan collapsed on to one of the sofas, her head spinning. "This is awful," she said. "All our hard work, all that money we were going to raise for Cheney Manor..."

"Look, Honey," Razina called out, checking a box at the far end of the line. "I think most of your crackers are OK. This box must have been out range of the rain."

"Great," Lynsey said sarcastically. "So we're left with a bunch of paper party favours. I'm so sure *that's* going to make the trip to mall worthwhile."

Rosie bit her lip. "She kind of has a point," she admitted. "It doesn't make much sense to go with just the few things we have left."

Dylan felt sick as she thought about disappointing the people at Cheney Manor. "Those poor kids," she said to Malory, who had just sat down beside her. "Now they won't get another minibus – or anything else, for that matter."

"Never mind," Malory said with a sigh. "I'm sure we can come up with a different fundraiser to help them."

Dylan didn't answer. She'd just seen her aunt stick her head in the door of the common room. It was a surprising sight to see her away from the stable yard – almost like seeing one of the ponies walk in. Ms Carmichael rarely came to any of the dorms.

"Hi," Dylan called. "What are you doing here?"

Her aunt smiled. "Ah, there you are, Dylan." She hurried over. "I just checked your room but you weren't there. I wanted to bring this back. Kelly found it on the seats in the indoor arena while we were cleaning up in there this morning. It's yours, isn't it?"

She held up a book. Dylan saw that it was the bird guide that Casey had borrowed, which she'd been carrying in her backpack.

"Oh," she said, taking the book. "Thanks. Casey must have forgotten it yesterday."

Her aunt said goodbye and left. Most of the other girls in the room hadn't even noticed she was there. They were still exclaiming over their spoiled project and wondering what to do next.

Dylan idly paged through the slightly damp pages of the bird book, hoping she wouldn't get in trouble with the librarian for its condition. She paused when she came to a spread about what birds eat. It included instructions on making bird treats to hang in your yard to attract birds.

"Hey," she blurted out, staring at the page. "I have an idea. Why don't we make bird decorations instead?"

"Huh?" Lani leaned down and grabbed the book. Her eyes lit up as she saw what Dylan meant. "That's perfect!" she exclaimed. "Look at this list of ingredients – nuts, cornmeal, peanut butter, oranges... That's just stuff you'd find in most kitchens."

"Like the cafeteria kitchen right here at Chestnut Hill, for instance?" Honey said with a smile as she and Malory crowded around to see the book too.

"And it wouldn't take long at all to make this stuff," Dylan said.

"Come on. Let's go show Rosie and the others." Lani headed that way.

Rosie thought it was a great idea. So did Mrs Herson. "I'll go speak to the catering staff right now," she said. "I'm sure they won't mind being raided for a special occasion. If we all work hard for the next couple of hours, we might still be able to get over to the mall today."

"You heard her," Rosie called out as the housemother hurried off. "Let's get organized so we're ready to start when she gets back. Dylan, since this was your idea, start dividing everyone into teams and tell them what they'll need to do."

"You can't be serious!" Lynsey exclaimed.

Dylan grinned at her. "What? You mean you don't want me telling you what to do? Tough luck."

Lynsey ignored her, staring at Rosie with her hands on her hips. "We're actually supposed to make, like, *bird food*? And that's going to be our great new fundraiser?"

"This could really work, Lynsey," Alexandra spoke up eagerly. "Last Christmas my family went to this big display garden, and they had a whole bunch of trees decorated all with edible ornaments for the birds. It looked really cool."

Lynsey appeared unconvinced. "Well, you guys can go ahead and waste your time playing with peanuts. I think I'll work on salvaging some of my ornaments."

"Suit yourself." Rosie didn't seem particularly interested in Lynsey's complaints. In fact, she looked downright excited. "As for the rest of us, let's get to work!"

However, this time Dylan couldn't just let Lynsey's obnoxious comments lie. She marched over to where Lynsey and Patience were picking through the rain-damaged boxes.

"Look," she said. "I know you're not thrilled about this birdseed idea. But how about showing some real teamwork for once?"

Lynsey narrowed her eyes at her. "What are you talking about?"

"You've been on my case this week about not being loyal to the jumping team." Dylan crossed her arms over her chest. "And maybe you were right. A little. Possibly. But the thing is, that had to do with a competition, and this doesn't. Or shouldn't."

"What's she talking about?" Patience asked Lynsey, wrinkling her nose.

Lynsey rolled her eyes. "How should I know? I don't speak Dylan's language, and I'm glad to say I never will."

"What I'm talking about is, we never should have turned this fundraiser into a competition," Dylan said. "We're supposed to be raising as much money as we can for the kids at Cheney Manor. *All* of us. This isn't a time to get personal and petty. Or competitive. It's not supposed to be about us. So I'd like to back off and cancel the bet. And I'm sorry for my part in messing things up with that stuff."

Lynsey raised an eyebrow and opened her mouth as if to say something snotty or argue back. But then she closed it again and shrugged.

"Whatever," she muttered. "Come on, Patience. I guess if everyone else is really going along with this crazy peanut idea, we might as well too."

"What?" Patience complained. She shot Dylan an annoyed look as she followed Lynsey over towards the others.

Dylan smiled as she watched them go. Lynsey hadn't exactly apologized for her role in their latest conflict, or even admitted she might have been even a tiny bit wrong.

But she'd come close enough. And Dylan was willing to take what she could get.

Three hours later, a new set of boxes was packed with dozens of bird-friendly decorations made of nuts, sunflower seeds, raisins, peanut butter and everything else Mrs Herson had found for them in the school kitchen. They'd also salvaged some of the ribbons and other pieces from the original designs to decorate the new ornaments and garlands. Christy Snowdon and Michelle Noble had even run out to the woods and cut some pine and juniper branches to make swags on which they could hang some of the edible stuff. Dylan thought the end result looked really nice – and smelled great, too!

When they got to the mall, the Christmas Fair was in full swing. The table they'd reserved was waiting for them, empty except for a plain red paper covering. But not for long. Soon the girls had unloaded their festive bird treats, along with Honey's crackers and the few other things they'd saved. They hung up the sign a couple of the seniors had drawn explaining their products and set out a bunch of smaller signs with prices as well as a stack of Cheney Manor brochures in case people wanted to make donations on their own.

There were plenty of other tables selling handmade crafts for humans, and even one with Christmas treats for dogs. But the Adams House table was the only one featuring ornaments for birds, and they were mobbed with customers from the start. All the girls were kept busy handing out change, explaining how they'd made the ornaments, and talking about Cheney Manor.

Dylan was counting out money for a little boy who'd just bought one of the juniper branches for his backyard when she spotted Casey walking towards their table. She was flanked by a couple of adults Dylan didn't recognize, a man and woman in their thirties.

"There you go," she told the little boy, handing him his change. "Merry Christmas!"

Casey walked up to the table, wearing her head scarf and earrings and smiling. "Hi, Dylan," she said. "We heard you guys were here today."

"Well, nobody told me you'd be here," Dylan replied. "But it's great to see you!" She echoed the second part in ASL for good measure.

"I didn't get to ask you yesterday," Casey said, suddenly looking anxious. "Your pony – Morello. Is he OK? I mean, after running through the woods and stuff..." Her cheeks went pink.

Dylan nodded. "He's fine. In fact, he told me it was the best adventure he's had in a while – really livened up the show." She winked.

Casey laughed. "Good! Um, thanks again for, you know, rescuing me."

"You're welcome."

The two adults had been looking over the selection of ornaments, but now they joined Casey in front of Dylan. "Would you like to pick something out, Casey?" the woman asked, signing as she spoke. "We can hang it outside your window when the holidays arrive."

"Um, thanks." Casey shot a bashful look at Dylan. "Dylan, this is Mr and Mrs Peel."

"Oh! So you're Dylan? It's so nice to meet you!" The man stuck out his hand and gave Dylan a friendly smile. "I'm Derek Peel, and this is my wife Jo. Thank you so much for all you've done for Casey."

"You're, um, welcome?" Dylan had no idea who the Peels were.

The woman, Jo, let out a laugh. "I'm guessing from

the confused look on your face that you're clueless about who we are," she said as if she'd read the thought bubble above Dylan's head. "No wonder – poor Casey only found out herself last night!"

"Oh!" Derek looked sheepish. "Of course. We've been so excited about this for so long... Anyway, we both volunteer at Cheney Manor as often as we can, and we've decided we're ready to take the next step and be foster parents."

Jo reached over and put an arm around Casey's shoulders. "And we have our heart set on Casey here," she said fondly. "We're spending the day together to see if she thinks she might be able to put up with us full-time."

Casey ducked her head and blushed. But Dylan could see that she looked happy.

"Wow, that's amazing!" she exclaimed. "So Casey would come live with you?"

"That's right," Derek said. "We have a house on Sixth Street – just a few blocks from Cheney Manor. So she'd still be able to see her friends there."

"And maybe still ride Tiptoe at Chestnut Hill?" Dylan asked hopefully.

"Oh, yes," Jo said. "We've already heard all about the wonderful Tiptoe! I can't wait to meet her. I rode a bit myself as a girl."

Casey nodded. "Derek is making me a bird feeder," she told Dylan. "So I can watch the birds whenever I want."

"That's awesome!" Dylan's heart swelled with

happiness for her new friend. She chatted with the Peels for a few more minutes, and by the time they left, laden down with several bird treats and half a dozen of Honey's crackers, she was completely convinced that they were the perfect new family for Casey.

She sighed blissfully as she watched the three of them disappear into the crowd. Malory leaned closer and gave her a hug.

"I couldn't help overhearing most of that," she said. "Sounds like Casey is going to have a great new life, huh?"

"Yeah." Dylan smiled and hugged her back. "I guess she was right. The Folly really does make wishes come true!"

If you enjoyed this, try this!

Chestnut Hill
The New Class

Lauren Brooke

By the author of *Heartland*

SCHOLASTIC

If you enjoyed this, try this!

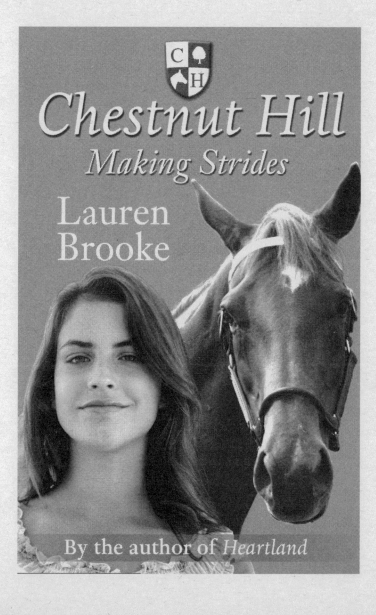

Chestnut Hill
Making Strides

Lauren Brooke

By the author of *Heartland*

If you enjoyed this, try this!

Chestnut Hill

Heart of Gold

Lauren Brooke

By the author of *Heartland*

SCHOLASTIC

If you enjoyed this, try this!

Chestnut Hill
Playing for Keeps

Lauren Brooke

By the author of *Heartland*

If you enjoyed this, try this!

Chestnut Hill

Team Spirit

Lauren Brooke

By the author of *Heartland*

If you enjoyed this, try this!

If you enjoyed this, try this!

Chestnut Hill
Chasing Dreams

Lauren
Brooke

By the author of *Heartland*

■ SCHOLASTIC

If you enjoyed this, try this!

Chestnut Hill
A Time to Remember

Lauren Brooke

By the author of *Heartland*